THE LAST WALTZ

By John Carruthers

ISBN 978-1-4116-9427-9

For my Guardian Angel. I love you Gran

And

For Tanja, who has helped make all my dreams come true

CHAPTER ONE

1.

A story has to begin somewhere and ours begins in a large hall. There is a large banner hanging from one wall to the other, bearing the legend "HAPPY 50th BIRTHDAY." The party is in full swing, people of all ages dancing in an embarrassing way to fairly modern music, some of them unaware of just how their bodies are supposed to move to it. The older ones are doing a slightly better job than their younger contemporaries.

The younger ones are more interested in hanging round the small bar that is serving various forms of alcohol - either that or the table full of food, which is being placed onto cardboard plates by the hungry attendees. Lots of comments are made about how they've "put on a good spread."

Two men walk onto the stage that dominates the hall, where a microphone is standing on its own. There is a DJ in the left hand corner, continuing to play music and seeming oblivious to the two newcomers. He has a specific job to do and he is caught up in the moment, not even caring how the crowd are taking to the music.

One of the men, John Kettle, who is the reason for everyone being here (it is his birthday), coughs lightly before tapping the microphone. The other, his best friend Martin Bates, gives a small smile.

"Is this thing on?" John enquires.

Martin gives a quick nod, as everyone turns round by the loud burst. The DJ realises that the time for speeches is here and the music stops in the middle of the song, even though, in a perfect world there would be no need for talk and the dancing could continue.

John seems to enjoy the limelight at that moment. Everyone is looking at him. "Thank you all for coming to my Birthday. This was such a surprise."

During these proceedings, his daughter, Maggie Hooper, is standing at the bar with a clear liquid in her glass. Her mother, Sarah Kettle, walks over, shaking her head slowly.

"That's a lot of crap. He overheard me talking to Ernest on the phone a couple of nights ago."

Maggie can't help but give her mother a quick smile for this comment.

John looks around in astonishment. How much of this is for dramatic effect, nobody can tell. "I didn't realise that I had so many friends."

There is a wave of laughter from people. During this pause, Martin walks over to the DJ. So begins the next phase of the birthday plan.

John continues. "I really don't know what to say. I am lost for words."

Sarah is now completely disregarding her husband. She stares at her daughter who is holding what appears to be a substantial glass of vodka. Her nose wrinkles up a little in disgust.

"Why are you drinking that straight?"

Maggie raises her glass to her face and looks through to her mother.

"I like to be able to see through my drink."

John is now standing at the microphone, his breathing heard by one and all. He has nothing more to say, but is rooted to the spot. Martin walks back over and John moves out of the way for him.

Martin seems much more comfortable in front of a microphone. "Thank you John. And now that you're fifty we thought that this music would be more to your taste."

Pennsylvania 6-5000 comes on and John gives a small smile. Martin walks quickly from the microphone as John watches the group. There is a loud clapping and John walks from the stage and to his wife.

"Dance with me, Sarah?"

Sarah lets out a giggle and nods. As they head off to the dance floor an old woman comes over to Maggie.

"You look just like your father."

Maggie, not sure how to take this, is about to say something to the old woman when Martin walks over to her.

"Won't you dance with me Maggie?"

Maggie gives him a nervous smile. "I can't really dance to this kind of music, Martin!"

In an effort to tempt her to change her mind, Martin starts dancing strangely in a shuffling motion in front of her.

"Come on, it'll be fun."

Maggie shakes her head. "I'm sorry."

Knowing when he is beaten, Martin nods. "It's okay. But I want a dance later."

He shuffles away with his bizarre dance.

"Won't somebody dance with me?"

Meanwhile, The old woman is still standing there, looking at Maggie. "You look just like your father."

It is at that moment that Keith Hooper, Maggie's husband, strides into the hall and looks around. He sees his wife and walks over to her. "Hi honey."

"Hi Keith. You missed my father's speech."

Keith kisses her on the lips, lightly. "Did he say much?"

"Lots."

Keith watches as the group dance to Pennsylvania 6-5000. "I love the music."

When the song finishes normal music resumes and John and Sarah come over. "Hello Keith."

Keith shakes John's hand. "Hi John. Happy Birthday!"

"Thank you."

Sarah picks that moment to interject. "When are you going to make us Grandparents?"

Keith gives an embarrassed laugh and Maggie blushes. "Mum!"

"We're working on it, Sarah," Keith replies.

John winks at Keith, who also starts to blush and looks at his feet.

"Buy you a drink, Keith?" His Father in Law asks.

Keith raises a hand and shakes his head. "No thank you sir. I'm driving tonight."

"But tonight's a party," Sarah feels she has to mention.

John looks out to the crowd. "There's Ernest."

Sarah grabs him by the arm. "Let's go and say hello."

John nods and turns to his daughter and Keith. "Excuse us."

John and Sarah leave. Maggie finishes her drink. "What you said about children?"

Keith looks at her. "Yeah?"

"Want to try when we get home?"

2.

Keith is in bed, waiting for Maggie. He can hear her brushing her teeth in the bathroom. It is very loud. Maggie comes out of the bathroom, wearing a nightdress, which she takes off very quickly, before climbing into bed. She switches off the lamp beside her bed. There is moonlight coming in through the window and the lack of lamplight does not make much difference. Keith turns to Maggie and they kiss. He moves a hand to one of her breasts and touches it lightly. She lets out a small moan. She kisses Keith harder. She moves closer to him. Keith moves on top of her and they are soon making love. Maggie does a great job of faking her orgasm - Keith is not the best of lovers. Keith comes very quickly and Maggie consoles him very well. No words are exchanged but it is obvious that the quick ending annoys Keith. Maggie has done the job of consoling her husband for his quickness on many an occasion. He rolls off of her and looks out of the window. There is the beginning of a tear in his eye and Maggie watches his back. She moves to touch and then decides not to.

3.

Maggie and Keith are sitting together, holding hands. The Doctor is looking at the two of them. "And how long have you been trying for a family for?"

Maggie looks to Keith. "Since we got married."

"Three years ago." Keith reiterates.

"And you're not using any form of protection?"

Keith looks confused.

"Contraception!"

Keith gives a look of understanding and then shakes his head.

"I'd like to run tests on the two of you."

Maggie nods. Keith looks nervous. "What kinds of tests do you want to run on us?"

"Tests to see if you are… capable of having children."

Keith and Maggie look at one another.

4.

Keith walks into the living room. He is tying his tie badly. Maggie is holding a letter in her hand. "We have to go and see the Doctor. He has the results of our tests."

"You'll have to go. I can't take the time off of work."

Maggie nods.

5.

The Doctor looks at Maggie. "I would have rather had Mr. Hooper here too."

"He couldn't get the time off of work."

"I'm afraid that he is the problem."

"What?"

"What?"

"You said he was the problem."

The Doctor nods. "Your husband has a very low sperm count. He cannot fertilise your eggs."

Maggie is silent for a few moments. She then decides to speak. "He wears briefs. Could that have anything to do with it?"

6.

Keith has five empty bottles of beer beside him, on the living room chair. Maggie is looking at him. He is drinking his sixth. Nothing is said.

7.

Maggie is lucky enough to have her dream job – she is a schoolteacher. She is standing in the classroom. She writes something on he blackboard. She then sits down and the children watch her. She does nothing but stare into space.

8.

Maggie is sitting in the staff room. There is a lot of cigarette smoke in the room. A couple of the teachers, names Matthew Carvel and Lynn Clements are talking. "Did you know that Belinda Eckerson wants to be a teacher?" He asks.

"I hope you talked the poor girl out of it?" Lynn replies.

"I think she'd do a great job."

"What do you think Maggie? You're just new to this. Would you wish it upon anyone?"

Maggie gives a small smile. "I'm sure there are worse jobs."

Matthew laughs but does not explain why.

"Are you going to the night out on Friday?" Lynn enquires.

"I don't know."

Matthew turns round to her. "You should go."

"It'll be great. It'll be your chance to get to know the others."

Maggie smiles weakly. "I'll see."

There is a pause for about thirty seconds.

"Okay, I'll go."

9.

In the pub, there are a group of teachers, all in a various state of drunkenness. Maggie does not look to be enjoying herself. She does not even see the figure watching her from the bar. Lynn turns to Maggie. "Are you having fun?"

Maggie smiles. "Of course I am."

The drinking continues. Matthew staggers over to the dance floor. He dances on his own for a few moments, as the others laugh at him. Lynn turns to Maggie. "Do you think that we should go and dance with him?"

Maggie shakes her head. "I'm fine. You go."

Lynn smiles and staggers over to Matthew. The two of them dance drunkenly. Another Teacher, Andrew Dodd, slides over to Maggie. "Tonight might be the night."

"I'm married. And I'm happy."

Andrew laughs sharply. Maggie winces at the sound of it. He points at Maggie and Matthew. "I mean with those two. They've fancied each other for years."

Maggie watches as the two of them dance closely. As they move in for a kiss, Maggie sucks the last of her drink, loudly from a straw.

10.

The Teachers are standing waiting for a Taxi in the rank just outside the pub. Martin is dancing in the queue. "Who wants to go to a club?"

Andrew laughs. "You'll never get in."

"I fucking will."

Maggie is staggering slightly. She has had too much to drink but she is by far the most sober of the group. "I'm going to walk home."

Lynn frowns. "Just wait for a Taxi."

Maggie shakes her head. "I'm not that far away. I'd be faster walking."

Matthew shouts over. "I think we should go to a club."

"You won't get in." Lynn feels the need to tell him again.

Matthew kisses her. "Let's have a private party then."

Maggie steps out of the queue. "I'll see you all on Monday."

Everybody waves and there is a multitude of "goodbyes". She walks away from them. Lynn looks to her friends. "I think she enjoyed herself."

11.

Maggie is striding down the main street. The figure that was watching her in the bar is following at a discreet distance. Maggie is completely oblivious to the person following her. She turns into an alley.

12.

Maggie is walking along the alley when she hears a noise behind her. She spins round. The Figure has put on a mask that covers his entire face, with the exception of his eyes and mouth. In the darkness it is difficult to make even this out. Maggie instantly feels scared, and she sobers up instantly.

"I… I don't have much money. But you can take it."

"I don't want your fucking money."

His voice is a croak. Maggie takes a step back. "I'll scream."

As fast as lightning, the masked man punches her in the face and she falls to the ground. Her nose is dripping blood and she looks up at him. He is on top of her in a second, ripping at her clothes. He puts a gloved hand over her mouth and stifles her screams. Maggie's eyes are open wide, darting from left to right. Her skirt is lifted up and her underwear is ripped from her. Everything seems to fade around her…

13.

…And she is standing in the middle of a stage… the stage her father stood on for his birthday, facing the hall, laid out for the festivities that were now long past. Her clothes are ripped at and she can feel blood all over her nose and mouth. The lights go off and a spotlight is put on her. Unable to control her voice she lets out a scream. But then another spotlight comes on and suddenly there is a man in a grey suit standing in the middle of the hall. He smiles at her. She looks down and her clothes are perfect and there is no feeling of blood on her face. Pennsylvania 6-5000 comes on and the man beckons her from the stage. Maggie comes from the stage and the spotlight follows her until both lights merge. The man puts one hand in one of hers and another on her hips.

"My name is David. May I have this dance?"

Maggie nods. "But what about..."

David gives a small shushing noise. "You don't want to be there right now."

The two of them begin to waltz round the room and the spotlight follows them for the duration of the song. Maggie feels...

Happy.

CHAPTER TWO

1.

Keith is sitting up in the bed. He is reading a book called *Broken Glass* by Stewart Charles. The incessant ticking of the clock serves as a distraction and every moment or so he looks up to see what time it is. He has a watch on but can never get used to any sort of jewellery, even his wedding ring and sometimes the best thing to do is ignore the things that annoy you. He shuts his book and looks out of the window. The ticking continues and Keith decides to resume reading.

2.

John and Sarah are sitting in chairs, facing one another. John is breathing on a photo of him in Police uniform and using a small cloth to wipe it. Sarah, too, is reading *Broken Glass.* They look at one another and then Sarah returns to his book. John breathes onto the photo again and gives it another wipe.

3.

The Police Station always seems so quiet at this time of night. Suddenly the sound of footsteps fills the air and Martin and Ernest walk round the corner, in Police uniforms and are striding up the corridor quickly. They are both very concerned indeed.

4.

They step into the office, the light of which is already on. Martin walks over to his desk and lays his hat down. Ernest does not know where to look. "I think that I should go to John and Sarah and tell them."

Ernest nods. "I don't envy you."

Martin is distracted, looking at a photo on the desk. It is of Martin, Ernest and John standing together. He looks at Ernest. "What was that?"

"I said I don't envy you."

"Has anyone gone to see her husband?"

Ernest shakes his head.

"I think you should go."

Ernest looks down at his feet. "I hate doing this."

"I know. But it has to be done."

5.

Keith has a glass of water in his hand and he proceeds to swallow it down with a number of small quick gulps. He places the glass on the table beside his bed and is about to return to his book when there is a knock at the front door.

6.

John is looking at Sarah as he places the photo back onto his mantelpiece.

"Sarah, I don't think that there's such a thing as a minor head injury."

Sarah opens her mouth to say something when the knocking at the front door interrupts her.

7.

Ernest is standing at the door. It opens and Keith is standing there, wearing a white gown. Keith has a look of concern on his face as soon as he sees Ernest standing there in uniform.

"I know you, don't I?"

Ernest nods. "I'm a friend of your father in law. Can I come in?"

Keith is making a sound in his mouth that makes it sound like he is sloshing saliva in his mouth. He gives a small swallow. "What's wrong?"

8.

Martin is standing at the door. It opens and Sarah comes to the door. She sees Martin and smiles. "Hi Martin. This is an unexpected surprise."

"Can I come in, Sarah?"

9.

Keith walks into the room and is followed by Ernest. He is pacing about. "I think you should sit down, Keith."

"I can't. It's about Maggie, isn't it? Is she okay?"

Ernest looks nervous.

"She's dead, isn't she?"

10.

Sarah and Martin walk into the room. John looks at him. "You're supposed to be on duty, not slacking off."

He gives a laugh and sees Martin is not joining him.

"I'm here on business John."

Sarah looks worried. "What's happened?"

Martin turns to her. "I think that you should sit down, Sarah."

John jumps up. "What the heck is this about, Martin?"

Martin looks sorry. "It's about Maggie."

Sarah lets out a squeal of shock. John stops in his tracks. "What's happened to her, Martin?"

Martin looks John in the eye. "She was walking home a couple of hours ago and tried to take a shortcut down a back alleyway."

John looks angry. "What the fuck happened to my daughter, Martin?"

"She was attacked and raped by an unknown assailant."

One of Sarah's hands flies to her mouth in shock. She is breathing heavily. Martin is still looking at John, who is no longer standing at full height. He is becoming limp to the extent that he looks ready to fold in half. "Is she…? Is she…? Dead?"

Martin shakes his head. "She's not dead, John. But she's severely traumatised. The bastard knocked her about a bit too. We haven't been able to get a great deal of sense out of her."

John stumbles backwards and falls to the floor. Sarah and Martin are by his side in a second. He is trying his hardest to breathe but cannot get any air. Martin looks at Sarah. "Phone an Ambulance!"

Sarah is up and away in a shot.

11.

Ernest and Keith are walking quickly along the corridor. Keith's hair is sticking up and he has just thrown old clothes on. His eyes are red and it is obvious he has been crying. They don't exchange any words as they stride along the corridor.

12.

Maggie is lying in the bed. She is in a bad shape. She is sleeping very soundly, considering the trauma that she has gone through. The door swings open and a Doctor walks in. Ernest and Keith follow.

"I would rather that you didn't stay too long. She's not in the best of shape."

"Thank you Doctor." Ernest replies.

The Doctor leaves. Keith walks to the bed. "Oh my God."

Ernest does not know where to look. Keith touches Maggie's cheek and she winces slightly. Her left eye flickers for a few seconds and then stops.

"Maggie, can you hear me?"

He gets no response to his answer.

"If I ever find the Bastard who did this to you, I'll kill him."

Ernest is looking at Maggie. There are tears beginning to form on his eyes and he wipes them away. He walks over to Keith and lays a hand on his shoulder. "I think that we should let her get some rest, Keith."

Keith shakes his head. "I want to stay with her."

"I understand, Keith. I really do."

The door opens again and Martin walks in. He has taken his tie off and his hat is missing. He looks at Maggie for a few seconds and looks at Keith. "I'm so sorry, Keith."

Keith gives a humourless smile. "She's alive and that's all that counts right now."

Martin gives an understanding nod.

"Where are John and Sarah?" Ernest asks Martin.

Keith spins round and puts a hand to his mouth. "Shit, I forgot about them. Do they know?"

Martin nods. The colour has drained from his face. "I went to the house."

"Where are they, Martin?" Ernest asks.

Martin shakes his head. "John collapsed when he heard the news. The Doctors think that it's a major stroke. It doesn't look good. Sarah is with him."

"Jesus Christ!" Ernest and Keith say in unison.

Martin looks out of the window. "It hasn't been a good night for any of us."

"I should go up and see John." Ernest says. He looks to Keith, as if for permission. Keith gives a brief nod and Ernest leaves. Martin and Keith regard each other for a moment.

"Jesus, Keith, I don't know what to say."

"I understand."

"We'll nail this Bastard. I promise you."

Ernest steps back into the room. "I forgot to ask, Martin. Where is John?"

"Sixth floor. Just ask a Doctor. I forget the room number."

Ernest nods and leaves again. But not before giving Maggie another quick look.

"Do you have any leads?" Keith asks.

Martin shakes his head. "It's too early yet. But someone's bound to remember seeing something. And maybe Maggie caught sight of her attacker."

"Rapist!"

Martin looks away from Keith.

"I'm sorry."

Martin puts a hand on his shoulder. "It's okay, Keith. I understand."

13.

Ernest walks into the Hospital room and sees John lying on the bed with lots of tubes attached to him, with things connected to his arms and tubes entering his mouth. Sarah turns round and looks at Ernest. He gives her a small smile. "Hi Sarah."

He looks at John and tries to hide the shock on his face. He fails.

"What are the Doctors saying?"

Sarah shakes her head. "It doesn't look good Ernest."

She stands up and hugs Ernest. She starts to cry. "I don't want him to die."

Ernest pats her back and looks at John. He does not even seem to be aware of their existence.

"The Doctors here are good. They'll pull him through."

John starts to mumble something, but he cannot be understood because of the tubes. Ernest is by his side in a second and Sarah is right behind him. "Honey?"

Ernest smiles at John. "Hi John."

John looks at him, but apart from that, there is no other response.

"I'll get a Doctor." Sarah says.

Ernest nods and Sarah is gone from his side.

"You'll get over this, John. And we'll find who did this to Maggie."

With the sound of that, John speaks, muffled because of the tubes. But it is obvious to Ernest that he is trying to say his daughter's name.

14.

Maggie is lying in her bed and her eyes pop open. "DAD!"

Martin and Keith speed over to her bedside. But her eyes are closed again. Keith looks at Martin. "Did that just happen or was it just a dream?"

15.

A Nurse comes in and looks at John seeing that he is awake. She looks at Ernest. "The Doctor will be here in a moment."

Ernest nods. Sarah is back again. John's eyes dart to her and he attempts to give her the thumbs up, giving up half way through. Sarah smiles but the tears in her eyes cause them to sparkle brightly. "You're going to be okay, John."

Ernest smiles and they all remain in the exact same position until the Doctor walks in. Then Ernest, the Nurse and Sarah turn round at the same time. The Doctor ignores them and walks over to John. He looks at him. He gives a reassuring smile and turns to the three. "I would like to check to see if Mr…" He looks at the chart. "…. Kettle has lost any use of his hands or his speech. Just standard things! But if I could ask the three of you to leave…

"I'm the Nurse." Says the Nurse.

This gets a quick smile from the Doctor. "Then you can stay. But you will both have to go. I'll keep you informed."

Ernest turns to Sarah. "We can go and visit Maggie."

Sarah nods. The Doctor adds. "That is a great idea. Go and visit Maggie."

He nods enthusiastically as the two of them leave. When the door shuts, the Doctor looks at the nurse. "Who's Maggie?"

16.

Sarah and Ernest walk into the room. Ernest smiles at Martin. "John is awake."

Martin smiles. Maggie's eyes snap open. She sits up. She looks at Sarah. "Mum?"

Sarah walks over and hugs her daughter. She pats her head. There is a wince of pain from Maggie.

"God, I'm sorry. Are you okay?"

Maggie nods. But her eyes reveal a different story. "I feel kind of sick. I feel kind of…"

Martin looks at her and she catches his stare.

"Invaded."

Martin gives her a sympathetic smile. "We know what you're going through. But we'll catch him. I swear to you that we will."

"You Dad collapsed when he heard the news. He's not in a good way." Sarah tells her.

Maggie nods. "I know."

Sarah cocks her head. "How can you know, Maggie?"

"He watched me dance." She gives a humourless laugh. "He watched me dance with David."

Keith looks confused. "Who the hell is David?"

CHAPTER THREE

1.

Keith walks out of a set of automatic doors with a couple of bags. Maggie walks out behind him and the brightness of the sun blinds her for a second. "Where did you park the car?"

Keith tries to point but he cannot because the bags are heavy. He ends up using his head to motion in the direction that they should go. Maggie follows him as they head into the car park.

2.

Keith opens the back door of the car and puts the bags in. He looks at Maggie. "Honey?"

She looks at him and smiles. "Yeah?"

"Are you okay?"

She nods with her eyes closed and the two of them get into the car.

3.

Back home, Maggie is sitting watching the television. Keith is looking at her with concern. She does not seem to acknowledge this. Then, out of the blue, she turns to him. "It almost seems like a waste of time me leaving the Hospital."

Keith is caught off guard by Maggie finally speaking him and is unable to speak for a second. "Why… Why honey?"

"Because I'm going to have to go up and see dad every night."

Keith nods.

"I'd like to get back to work on Monday as well."

"They said that there was no rush."

"Have you ever watched daytime television?"

4.

Maggie and Keith walk into the ward where father is being kept and see Sarah standing there. She turns and smiles a humourless smile. "The Doctor thinks that John won't ever talk again."

Sarah bursts into tears. She walks to Keith, who gives her a hug. She looks at Maggie.

"The Doctor was nice. But he said he would be surprised if John ever regained the ability to move. He's paralysed from the neck down."

Maggie is standing in shock. "But you said that you heard him talk?"

Sarah shakes her head. She looks at her feet and turns back to John. Keith looks at Maggie.

5.

Keith is lying asleep in bed. Maggie looks at the far wall, with the bedside lamp on. She blinks every so often, but not much else.

6.

Lynn, Matthew and Andrew are sitting, drinking coffee and smoking in the staff room. The door opens and Maggie steps inside. Lynn is the first one to see her and puts her coffee down. She gets up and hugs Maggie. The men do not know what to do and put their cups down and pick them up again and look nervous.

Matthew is the first to speak. "I… I didn't think that we would see you here for a while Maggie."

Maggie smiles. "There was nothing to do around the house."

"You should have taken more time off, Maggie", Lynn tells her.

Maggie nods. "I know. But if I don't keep my mind busy, I just keep remembering that night."

"I suppose that means you won't be going to any more nights out then…" Andrew says. He realises this was the worst statement he could have made and a look of apology appears on his face. "Oh Christ, I didn't mean to say it like that, Maggie."

Maggie smiles again. "Don't worry about it Andrew."

Andrew looks relieved by Lynn is looking at him angrily. Maggie continues. "And of course I'll be going to the next night out."

"You will?" Andrew asks.

"Yes. Because of the laws of averages!"

Andrew and Matthew look confused.

"Think about it. What are the chances of getting raped two nights out in a row?"

Andrew and Matthew laugh despite themselves and Lynn gives her a smile. But, as Lynn is walking back to the table, she misses that Maggie is not okay at all as the mask she is hiding behind drops for a second.

7.

Sarah and Maggie are sitting at John's bedside together. "Keith told me that you have gone back to school."

Maggie nods.

"Did the kids not wonder where you were?"

"I'm sure that there were rumours. I'm sure some of them were close to the mark as well." Maggie looks out of the window, which is where John is facing. "I don't know why, but kids always seem to be good at working things like that out."

8.

Back home, Keith is reading a book. He turns to Maggie, who is just staring into space again. "You okay?"

Maggie nods.

"We've not talked about this."

Maggie shakes her head. "I'm not ready. Not yet!"

Keith puts a hand on her wrist. He smiles. "I promise that I'll stick by you."

Maggie nods. "I know you will."

"I hope that you do."

9.

Keith is tying his tie in front of a mirror. Maggie walks out and looks at him. "That was mum on the phone."

Keith looks at her. "What was she saying?"

"The Hospital is beginning to think that it might be okay for dad to go home soon."

Keith smiles. But then he stops. "Is that good?"

Maggie nods. "I'm not sure. I think so."

She comes over and hugs him. Keith appreciates the closeness… something that has been missing since the rape.

10.

Sarah is sitting by John's bed. Keith walks in with Maggie. "Hi Mum."

"Hi honey."

"You'll be glad that you won't have to be coming up here every day and night soon." Keith says.

Sarah shakes her head. "It's only been three and a half weeks. I would have come up here for three and a half months or three and a half years or however long I had to."

Keith looks to the window. "I'm sorry."

"Sorry, I wasn't meaning to snap. I was just stating a fact."

"Do they know yet when he'll be coming home?" Maggie asks.

"Soon!"

11.

Keith wakes up and turns in the bed to see that Maggie is not there. He is sitting up in a shot and looking around the room.

12.

Maggie is kneeling in front of the toilet bowl. She is breathing heavily and a yellow liquid drips from her lip. She wipes it with the back of her hand.

13.

Maggie walks into the classroom slowly and looks at the children. They are all watching her intently. She turns to the black board and starts scribbling something down.

14.

Sarah is holding John's hand. His eyes are darting from left to right and he looks helpless. When Maggie enters the room, his eyes fix on her and a smile plays on his lips.

15.

Keith wakes up and turns in the bed to see that Maggie is once again not there.

16.

Lynn walks into the toilet and walks over the mirror. She looks up her nose and takes out a small pair of tweezers from her purse. She is about to pull a hair from her nose when the door opens and Maggie walks in. She tries to act naturally and hides the tweezers from view. "Lynn, we need to talk."

17.

A waiter comes over to the table where Maggie and Lynn are sitting. Lynn smiles at him. "We haven't really decided what we want yet."

"I'm having a jacket potato with… cheese."

She licks her lips.

"Okay… I'll have that too. And can we have two cups of coffee please?"

The waiter leaves.

"So what is this about? I was supposed to be going back to Matthew's place at lunchtime."

"And I bet it wasn't for lunch."

"Martin says that I make him feel like a schoolboy."

Maggie and Lynn giggle.

"He's in the right profession. He could get one whenever he wants."

Lynn laughs as the coffee arrives.

"So why did you bring me to lunch?"

Maggie gets serious. "I had to tell someone." She stops for a second. "I mean, I might be wrong. But it's paranoia. And everything seems to point to it."

18.

Maggie is brushing her teeth. She flushes the toilet when she is finished and a yellowish liquid swirls away.

19.

Lynn seriously listens to every word that Maggie says. "And I'm a week and a half late for my period."

Lynn nods. "You need to go and see a Doctor."

Maggie nods too. "But what if I am? A Doctor told us that he couldn't."

"So that means…"

Maggie nods again.

"Jesus fucking Christ."

There is a family with a child at the next table and the mother looks at Lynn. "Our son's here."

The father shakes his head and closes his eyes. "For god's sake, don't make a scene."

"I think I have the right. If you're going to speak like that, please have the courtesy to check to see if there are sensitive ears about."

"I'm sorry."

"I don't want sorry. I just don't want my children hearing words like that."

"Did you say children?"

"Yes I did."

"I thought you only wanted one."

"I don't think that this is the place to discuss it."

"We can't afford another kid."

"Little Malcolm will need a playmate soon."

Lynn mouths "Malcolm" to Maggie and the two of them nearly burst out laughing.

20.

Keith is fixing his tie in front of the mirror again when Maggie walks in. He smiles and she smiles back.

"You've got something in your teeth."

Keith kisses her on the cheek and walks away from the mirror. She looks at her reflection and sees a small yellow solid piece of vomit. She picks it out with her fingernail and drops it into a paper basket. She walks to the phone. She opens up the phone book and starts dialling a number that is listed. She waits for a few seconds.

"Hi... Good morning... I'm looking for an appointment... His name is Doctor... Quinn... No Quigley...No, she'll do fine. Three O clock tomorrow? That's terrific, thanks. My name is Margaret Hooper. H-O-O... Yes, that's right. That's brilliant... Three o' clock tomorrow. Thank you very much. Bye... Bye..."

Keith walks back in a few moments later." Are you ready? I have to go."

21.

Keith wheels John into the living room. He puts him beside the chair that John used to sit in. Sarah kisses her husband on the cheek. "Welcome home."

"Maggie will be over tonight. She couldn't get the time off of work." Keith tells them.

22.

Maggie is sitting in front of the doctor.

"I'll get a nurse to take some blood from you. Also…" the doctor hands her a small plastic container. "I need a urine sample. But it has to be the first time you pass water that morning. Come back in with it tomorrow."

"Can I come in before work? I don't like the idea of walking about with a container of pee in my bag. That's just asking for trouble."

"No problem!"

Maggie gets up and shakes the doctor's hand. "Thank you Doctor."

She walks to the door and turns round.

"Oh yeah, just one more thing, Doctor."

"Yes?"

"How long will it take to find out the results?"

"About five days!"

This surprises Maggie. "Five days! But you can get the tests from the chemist that tells you in two minutes."

The Doctor nods. "Yes, but ours are one hundred percent accurate. Do you know which room the nurse is in?"

"Second on the left?"

The Doctor nods. "Second on the left."

23.

Lynn is washing her hands when Maggie bursts in. Her eyes are wide and Lynn cannot tell if she is excited or scared.

"Lynn! I'm pregnant!"

CHAPTER FOUR

1.

Sarah walks into the living room with Maggie and Keith. Ernest and Martin are already standing there with glasses of red wine in their hands. John is sitting in his wheelchair, regarding Maggie.

"Hi dad!"

Maggie goes over and kisses her dad's cheek. He gives a close approximation of a smile.

"How are you feeling Maggie?" Ernest asks.

Maggie nods. "I'm doing fine."

"Glad to hear it."

Martin takes a large gulp from his glass of red wine. "I'm glad too. Some people can be traumatised by what you went through for the rest of their lives."

Ernest looks at Martin. "For God's sake, Martin!"

Maggie shakes her head. "It's okay."

Martin looks apologetic. "I'm sorry, Maggie. I didn't mean anything by it."

Keith is standing there, looking at John. He tries to stop but seems to keep looking at his father in law. Sarah interrupts him with a glass of red wine. He shakes his head. "I'm the driver tonight… But Maggie will have it."

Maggie turns to her Mother and smiles. She shakes her head. "No thanks, Mum!"

Sarah shrugs and starts sipping at it. Keith looks at Maggie, who smiles nervously.

2.

Keith is sitting in bed, reading. Maggie steps in and walks towards the bed. She gives a small squeal of pain and gives a short hop. She looks down and we see that she has just stepped on a coat hanger. Keith jumps out of bed and picks it up. Maggie sits on the bed. "How the hell did that get on the floor?"

Keith shrugs. "I don't have a clue." Keith keeps hold of the coat hanger. "Why didn't you have a drink tonight?"

"Why?"

"You had the freedom to drink. I was driving. You could have knocked yourself out with it."

Maggie shrugs. "I just wasn't in the mood."

Keith shakes his head. "You're always in the mood for red wine."

"Not tonight!"

Keith looks at her. "What's wrong?"

Maggie shakes her head. "Nothing!"

"If you don't tell me then I can't help you."

Maggie looks close to tears and Keith looks at her sympathetically. "Is at about the rape?"

Maggie shakes her head, pauses, and then nods. She feels the pulse of the blood dripping from her foot. "I'm pregnant, Keith."

Keith just looks at her and his arms rises, bringing up the coat hanger. He doesn't seem to know why he did this and his arm drops to his side again. Maggie thinks the pulsing in her foot will drive her mad.

3.

Martin walks into the office and sees a letter on his desk. He picks it up and opens it. He starts reading.

4.

Keith is standing in the room. Maggie walks in. She cannot look at him.

"We have to talk about this, Maggie!"

5.

There is a knock at the door, as Ernest is looking through files and he looks up. Martin walks in.

6.

Keith looks imploringly at Maggie. "What are we going to do about this?"

Maggie tries to blink the tears out of her eyes. "What do you mean?"

"Are we going to abort it or what?"

7.

Martin throws the letter onto Ernest's desk. Ernest looks at it. "What is this?"

Martin looks annoyed. "They're trying to give me John's job."

Ernest looks at him.

8.

Maggie looks at Keith with a mixture of sadness and anger. "What?"

"This is the child of the man who raped you."

Maggie nods. She is beginning to quiver and cry. "I know."

"We can't possibly keep it. You're not thinking about keeping it."

Maggie wipes the tears from her eyes. "I don't know what I'm thinking right now."

9.

Ernest finishes reading the letter and then looks at Martin. "I assume that you're going to take it."

"I can't take it. That's John's job. It'll look like I'm taking advantage of a tragedy."

10.

Keith walks to the window. "I cannot believe that you are even fucking thinking about this."

Maggie is hysterical at this point. "I'VE ALWAYS WANTED CHILDREN KEITH. THIS MIGHT BE MY LAST CHANCE."

Keith spins round. "IT'S NOT MY FAULT THAT I CAN'T HAVE KIDS IS IT?"

"I didn't say that."

"So that's what it is, you're so desperate to have children that you'll keep a rape child?"

Maggie is almost choking with tears.

"You'll fucking resent this kid."

11.

Martin is sitting opposite Ernest now. "What if I always fucking resent the fact that I got the job this way?"

Ernest shakes his head. "I'm sure that John would rather you got the job than some wet behind the ears university graduate."

Martin nods. "You have a point. I'll think about it."

12.

Maggie is facing away from Keith now. Keith puts his hands on Maggie's shoulders. He is calmer now. "Honey, I'm sorry. But you know that I'm right."

"I can't make a decision like this over night."

Keith nods, despite the fact that Maggie cannot see him.

"Just give me time."

"I'm sorry honey. I'll be here for you. But the choice is down to you. It's your choice."

Maggie nods and walks out of the room. A few moments later Keith looks at the door. "And it's your kid."

13.

Maggie and Lynn are standing at the mirrors, not paying any attention to their reflections. "He had no fucking right to speak to you like that."

Maggie looks at her reflection and blinks a few times. "Maybe he does."

"Look, Maggie, he has to give you space."

"He was right. I do have to make a decision."

"If you need someone to talk to then you know that I'm here."

Maggie nods and smiles sadly. "Thanks Lynn."

14.

Martin walks up the path and knocks on the door. He waits for a few moments before Sheila opens.

"Hi. Can I come in?"

Sheila nods.

15.

John is sitting in the exact same position that he was in the night before. He does not seem to have moved. Martin walks in and gives him a small wave. John cocks his head slightly and blinks a few times. Sheila walks in. "I was just about to give John breakfast."

Martin shakes his head. "This won't take long."

Martin walks to John and takes one of his hands. John looks at him.

"John, I need to ask you something."

16.

Maggie looks at Lynn. "What should I do?"

17.

Sheila walks over to Martin and John.

"I have been offered your job, John. I don't know what to do."

John looks at Martin. He gives an attempt at a smile. Sheila puts a hand on Martin's shoulder. "They couldn't have picked a better person for the job."

18.

Lynn washes her hands in a sink, seemingly just for something to do. "Do you want to know what I think?"

Maggie nods.

"You have always wanted a kid. Keith has always wanted a kid too."

"Yes."

"Then this is an opportunity. You have to take it."

Maggie shakes her head. "But it's a rape baby."

Lynn nods. "Yes. You will have to live with the fact that you have been raped for the rest of your life. There is nothing that you can do about that. But if you have this child then you have the chance to make something good from what happened." Lynn smiles. "That might make what happened to you almost bearable."

Maggie is clearly thinking about this. "You're right. But there is not just me to think about. I have to consider Keith as well."

"Keith should grow up."

19.

Maggie is very restless looking and she is moving around a little. Keith wakes up and turns round to look at her. She mouths something.

"What is it?" Keith asks her.

Maggie turns away from Keith. Her face has a thin sheen of sweat over it.

20.

Maggie is standing on the stage once more. She is wearing the same clothes as the night she was raped but they are not ripped or damaged in any way. The lights are on and Maggie is looking at something. She smiles. "Who are you?"

The man in the grey suit, David, is standing at the other end of the hall. He does not say anything, but motions her to the door that he is standing beside. Maggie shakes her head. "I'm not coming over until you tell me who you are."

David puts a finger to his mouth to shush her. Maggie walks down the steps and starts towards him. "Who are you?"

Maggie is over to David in just under a moment. John is standing beside her. "I stood here and I watched you dance."

Maggie smiles and hugs her father. "Dad, it's so good to hear your voice."

"I'll always be here in the hall to talk to you."

Maggie turns to David, who is smiling.

"He keeps me company. Being unable to communicate with the outside world is a hard thing to do." John finishes.

Maggie nods. When she looks back to where her father was, he is gone. "Where has he gone?"

"Exploring!"

"Who are you?"

David shows a clenched fist to Maggie. It opens up and there is a key.

"Take it."

Maggie takes the key and holds it in her hand. It looks like a normal key but Maggie is amazed by it. "It's beautiful."

David nods.

"But what is it for?"

"You have been presented with a key. Keys are used to unlock doors."

Maggie is still looking at the key. "What door does this key unlock?"

David looks at the door that he is standing beside. "It is a door that you may not want to open."

Maggie walks to the door and puts the key in the lock. She looks at David.

"I'm going to find out who you are."

David nods. "Yes, you are. Are you sure that you want to open the door?"

Maggie nods and turns the key. She opens it. The masked man who raped her is standing on the other side. Maggie screams and the figure jumps at her. She is on the floor, kicking at him. David watches as this happens.

"Do you understand what you have been told?"

Maggie nods and finds she is alone in the room.

21.

Keith is watching Maggie with a look of dread. Her eyes flip open. She is breathing heavily and is looking directly at him.

"You've decided to keep it, haven't you?"

Maggie nods and there is silence for a moment.

CHAPTER FIVE

1.

Keith is standing alone and there is a sound like gusting wind blowing through his ears. He has an expressionless look on his face and seems to be unaware of his surroundings and the noise.

2.

Maggie is looking at Keith, who has the expressionless look on his face. "Keith!"

Keith snaps out of it and looks at Maggie as if he has just noticed her. "Sorry, what?"

Maggie looks concerned. "We haven't really spoken about this."

"We haven't spoken about what?"

"We haven't spoken about me keeping the baby."

Keith shakes his head. "I don't know what there is to talk about. You've made your choice."

"But you're not okay with it."

Keith stands up from the chair he was sitting on. "I don't know if I'm okay or not with it."

He walks to the door.

"Where are you going?"

"Out for a drink."

Maggie stays in the same position as the door slams.

3.

Keith is sitting with a group of people and drinking a lot. He is enjoying himself and doesn't even want to think about having to go home right now.

4.

Keith staggers out of the pub and waves goodnight to a couple of the people he was with before walking as normal as he can, with his head looking at his feet.

5.

Keith walks down a road and finds himself amongst a collection of prostitutes. A middle-aged woman with peroxide blonde hair steps out. "You looking for business love?"

Keith shakes his head. "I'm just trying to get home."

He receives a smile from the woman. "Are you sure?"

Keith nods. The woman steps away and Keith stumbles on, passing more prostitutes. Some of them look like they should still be at school while others look like they should be collecting their pensions. An attractive prostitute with short dark hair is the next one to stop Keith. She seems a bit unsure of herself. "Are you looking for business?"

Keith looks at her. He seems to be debating it. He then shakes his head. "I'm married."

The prostitute smiles at this. "Most of them are."

Keith shakes his head again. "I love my wife."

"You came down here for a reason."

"It's a faster route home."

"Have you ever come down this way before?"

Keith shakes his head.

"It's fifteen pounds for hand, twenty pounds for oral, or twenty-five pounds for full."

"Twenty-five pounds for full sex?"

The Prostitute nods.

"That's cheap."

"Well then, are you going to go or come with me?"

6.

Keith and the Prostitute are in a dark corner. She takes out a condom. "Take your trousers and boxers down and put this on."

Keith is nervous as he undoes his trouser buckle.

"There's nothing to worry about."

"What if the Police come?"

"It's me they arrest, not you."

Keith stops. "I can't do this. Not outside!"

The Prostitute smiles at him. "We could go back to my house."

"That would be better."

"But it'll cost more."

"How much will it cost?"

"Fifty! But it's for an hour."

Keith is thinking about it.

"How many times do you think you can come in an hour?"

7.

Keith and the Prostitute are in the back of a Taxi. They are speaking in low voices so as not to let the driver know what is going on. "Is this an hour from when we get into the house or from when we met?"

"From when we get into the house."

The light on the Taxi Driver's clock is saying 1:12 "So where were you?" He asks.

"What?" Keith asks.

"Where were you?"

"It was a works night out." The Prostitute says.

"You both work together?"

The prostitute nods. "That's how we met each other. We've been going out for… how long, honey?"

"About nine months!"

"Great, I love to see two people in love. It's great. Look at me. Married for fifteen years. Never regretted it once. Not once! Not even when her sister came onto me! What a fucking story that was."

8.

Keith is looking at the flats.

"Pay me now."

Keith looks at her. "What?"

"Pay me before we go up."

"Don't you trust me?"

"I had an old guy once, got half way up the stairs and changed his mind and ran off. I like to be paid before we get to the house now. It's sort of an incentive to stop you from changing your mind."

9.

The Prostitute and Keith walk into the bedroom. She flicks on a lamp with a red bulb and walks to the window.

"It's a cold one tonight."

She puts on a fire.

"Do you want a cup of tea before we start or something?"

Keith does not know what to do and nods.

Then:

The Prostitute's head moves up from his lap and she kisses his chin.

"What do you want to do?"

Then:

Keith is on top of her when he hears the front door open. Keith stops. "What the fuck is that?"

"That's my pal. I share a flat with her. She keeps out of my way when I bring business home and I keep out of hers."

Keith continues.

Then:

Keith is taking the Prostitute from behind when she looks at the clock. It says ten past two. Keith is close to coming by the looks of it.

"Hold it."

"What?"

"It's been more than an hour."

"What?"

"You came here at one. You've been over an hour."

"We didn't get a taxi until after one."

The Prostitute jumps out of the bed. "You're into the second hour. You owe me double."

"Bullshit."

"You owe me double."

Keith looks annoyed.

"I'm not paying you double. This is fucking bullshit."

The Prostitute walks out of the room and Keith gets his clothes together and starts to get dressed. "Double!"

The Prostitute walks back in with a large man, who is obviously her pimp or something like one. Keith turns round and sees him. He has a look of shock in his eyes but managed to hide it quite well after the initial shock.

"Hi there." The man says.

Keith raises his hand up in a still wave. "Hi."

"Could you do me a favour?" She asks the newcomer.

"Yeah, what is it?"

"This guy here…" She looks at Keith. "What's your name?"

"Gordon!"

"Yeah, Gordon owes me double because he kind of spent longer with me than he should have."

Keith is panicking and is wondering how this is going to end.

"It was a mistake and now the poor guy has to pay me double. But he has no cash on him."

The Pimp nods.

"Could you walk him to a cash machine and get it for him. I'm going in for a bath."

"Yeah, I think I could manage that."

Keith lets out a sigh. The Pimp smiles in a very untrustworthy manner. "I'll just get my jacket."

He walks out of the room.

"I don't owe you double!"

"Look, if you don't pay me, it's him you're fucking with, not me."

She gives a sad smile.

"It's not my fault. But he'll take you to the bank and he'll just take the fifty. He's not going to mug you or anything. He's not that bad."

Keith nods and the Pimp walks in again with his jacket on. "You ready?"

10.

Keith gets money out of the bank and hands it to the Pimp.

"Thanks."

"Tell her that I won't be coming back to her again."

The Pimp grabs him by the scruff of the neck. "Don't get cocky. I've been nice. But I get nasty really easy." He lets Keith go. "I'm sure her heart will be bleeding."

The Pimp walks away and leaves Keith standing, shaking. When the guy is out of sight, Keith lets out a gasp of air. "I get nasty really easy? Who the hell talks like that?"

11.

Keith climbs out of a Taxi and walks to the house. The upstairs light is on. He looks up at the window.

12.

Keith steps into the room and sees Maggie is still awake.

"Where the hell have you been?"

"That's my business."

He sits on the bed and tries to take his shoes off. He manages one and then lies on his back, letting out a gasp. He lies there for a few moments and Maggie looks at him. After a short while, he begins snoring.

13.

Maggie has a piece of toast in her hand and is looking through the mail. She opens a letter and looks at it. She scans something and walks swiftly out of the room.

14.

Keith is sitting on a chair, looking annoyed with life in general. Maggie storms in, holding the letter in the air. "One hundred and thirty pounds!"

Keith looks at her. "What?"

"You're night out a fortnight ago. Do you remember it?"

Keith nods slowly.

"That night you managed to take one hundred and thirty pounds out of the bank."

Keith continues to look at her but it is obvious that he wants to look elsewhere.

"What the hell did you spend that kind of money on in a night?"

Keith starts swallowing as his mouth has dried up.

"Well?"

15.

Keith is sitting, looking at a quarter full pint glass. Daniel, one of his pals, is sitting there.

"She's just pissing me off right now."

"No fucking wonder mate, keeping that kid."

Keith puts his thumb and index finger close together. "I am this fucking close to leaving the bitch."

Daniel takes a drink of his pint.

"Why don't the fuck don't you?"

Keith shakes his head. "I don't really think I love her any more. She's just fucked me up."

"I've got a flat going in my building. Why don't you just fuck of tomorrow and rent it? It's only a couple of hundred a month. It's not the fucking Ritz but it does the fucking damage."

"You know what, I fucking will."

16.

Maggie walks into the room, annoyed. She is dripping wet. She sees a letter sitting on the table with her name on it and walks over to it. She opens the letter and starts to read.

CHAPTER SIX

1.

Maggie is sitting on the bed with her legs crossed. She is crying. There is a noise of thunder outside.

2.

Maggie walks in and tries to act as if she is okay. Lynn is the only one there. "What's wrong?"

Maggie shakes her head. "Nothing!"

"Don't lie to me. What's wrong?"

"Keith's left me."

Lynn's eyes widen. "What?"

Maggie starts to cry. "He's been acting strangely since I told him that I'm keeping the baby. And a few weeks ago one hundred and thirty pounds disappeared from the bank. He couldn't have drunk all that. He was probably putting down a deposit for a flat or something."

Lynn shakes her head. "That Bastard…"

Maggie wipes her eyes. "I didn't want to talk about this in work."

"Are you still going keep the kid?"

Maggie nods. "Yes. I need this child. I think that it's going to lead me somewhere."

Lynn looks confused. "What do you mean?"

"I've had these dreams."

Lynn looks interested.

"There's this man called David. He's my protector. He's almost like a guardian angel.

"Cool!"

Maggie smiles. "He made me forget about the rape. I don't remember anything about the pain or anything. It's just a blank and David danced with me."

"You've never told me this before?"

Maggie shakes her head. "I've never told anybody. I can also talk to my dad through him. It was so good to hear his voice again."

Lynn nods. The emotion Maggie is feeling right now is catching her too.

"Something he said convinced me that I had to keep this child."

"What did he say?"

Maggie shakes her head. "I don't really remember. All I remember is speaking to my father and opening a door. There was something behind the door that I didn't want to see."

"What was it?"

"I think it was the man who raped me."

Lynn lets out a long sigh. "Jesus Christ!"

"Lynn, I'm convinced that if I have this baby, I'll find out who the bastard who raped me was."

"How?"

"I don't know yet."

3.

Maggie is walking out of the house and Andrew pulls up in his car. She is beginning to show as being pregnant. He gets out of the car and opens the passenger door for her. She walks to the car. "Are you sure this is no problem?"

Andrew smiles. "No problem at all!"

4.

Maggie teaches the children. The children watch her intently but a couple of the girls cannot help but look at her growing stomach.

5.

Maggie is drinking a coffee in her living room while Lynn has a glass of wine. "This is nice."

"Everyone's been so great. Andrew comes by every day and drives me to work."

"He fancies you."

Maggie shakes her head. "No, he doesn't."

Lynn laughs. "Do you fancy him?"

Maggie shakes her head. "No! And he's just being sweet. He's a gentleman." She shows her hands to Lynn. "Anyway, how can you fancy someone with podgy fingers?"

"There's nothing wrong with your fingers."

"When I tried phoning you last night I think I got through to someone in China."

Lynn laughs. "Honestly. I hit about three numbers at once."

6.

Maggie is reading a book. The ticking of the clock is very loud and it distracts her occasionally.

7.

Matthew and Andrew are sitting in the staff room.

"So how are you and Lynn getting on?"

Matthew nods. "Great! The sex is brilliant."

Andrew waves a hand at him. "Enough!"

Matthew laughs. "So how's your love life?"

"What's one of them?"

The door opens and Maggie walks in, looking even more pregnant. "Andrew can I ask you a favour?"

Andrew nods.

"I'm going to one of those pregnancy classes tonight where they teach you how to breathe and stuff."

"For a teacher, your grammar is terrible." Matthew says.

"Well I heard you've got a small dick."

Matthew nods. "Well, you got me there."

Maggie smiles. "Anyway, I need a partner. They don't supply one. Could you come?"

Andrew nods but he is a bit worried looking. "Yeah, no problem."

Maggie laughs. "It doesn't mean you have to attend the birth or anything. It's at seven."

"I'll pick you up at six thirty."

"Thanks."

Maggie leaves. Matthew looks at Andrew. "She fancies you."

Andrew shakes his head. "No she doesn't."

"You fancy her, don't you?"

Andrew looks at him astonished. "I don't believe you sometimes."

"God you do fancy her."

There is a moment or two of silence. Then Matthew asks. "How the hell can you fancy someone with podgy fingers?"

8.

Maggie and Andrew do various exercises along with other couples. One of the couples comprises of two women and they are doing the exercises. "You could have brought Lynn. It doesn't have to be a guy."

Maggie smiles. "I was talking to them last week. The pregnant girl is called Angela. She was engaged to the other woman's brother and she got pregnant. But then she found out she was more attracted to her fiancé's sister and the two of them ran away together."

"Oh!"

9.

Maggie carries a cup of coffee over to the table and hands it to Andrew.

"I enjoyed myself tonight."

"Good. You can come next week too if you want."

Andrew nods. "I'd like that."

He takes a drink of coffee and looks at Maggie. "Do you hear from Keith at all?"

Maggie shakes her head. "I haven't heard from him in months." She feels tears well up in her eyes and tried to fight them. "I can't believe that he just upped and left me."

Andrew shakes his head. "It's his loss. You're a great person and he's stupid to let you go."

There is silence.

"Do you have any ideas for names?"

Maggie nods. "Lynn and I have talked about it. If I have a girl then I'm going call her Maggie."

"Yeah?"

Maggie smiles. "Yeah. It's a vanity thing."

"And what if it's a boy?"

Maggie takes a slug of coffee and looks at Andrew. "I'm going to call him David."

10.

Andrew is driving home. He is on his own. He is listening to I ONLY WANT TO BE WITH YOU on the radio and is singing along to it. He turns and looks at the passenger seat. Maggie is sitting there. She smiles at him. He smiles back and looks at the road again. He looks back and she is gone. He looks disappointed. When he looks again, Matthew is sitting there. "You don't just fancy her mate, you're totally in love with her."

Andrew looks at the road. He is alone again.

"Oh my God, I'm totally in love with her."

11.

Maggie is sitting on a chair in her parents living room, even more heavily pregnant. John is trying to smile at her but still cannot master it. Sheila looks at Maggie. "Have you heard from Keith?"

Maggie shakes her head.

"I can't believe that Keith would do that. He was so nice. John and I were proud to have him as a son in law."

"Mum, every time I'm up here, I have to listen to this."

Sheila looks sad. "I'm sorry Margaret."

Maggie bites her lip. "Mum, I'm sorry."

Sheila smiles. "It's okay."

"I've been snappish of late."

Sheila nods. "It won't be long now."

Maggie pats her stomach lightly. "It won't be long now."

12.

Maggie walks into her living room with letters. She puts them on a table. She looks unwell and very pregnant. She opens a letter that she still has in hand. She reads it. She reacts as if she has just been kicked. She drops the letter and clutches her stomach. She reels back and bangs off of the table. "Oh Christ, no."

She looks down at the letter, which informs her that Keith wants to start divorce proceedings immediately. Maggie's face is creased up in pain. "I can't lose you now."

13.

Maggie is sitting up in bed when Sheila comes in with Ernest and Martin. Sheila is crying. There is a pause for a moment. "I'm a Grandmother."

Maggie nods. She is emotional too. "She's six weeks early! I was convinced when I went into labour that I was losing her."

Sheila smiles. "You were six weeks early too honey."

Maggie cocks her head. "Was I?"

Sheila nods. "I thought that you knew. I was so scared. Back then it was a lot more serious than it is now."

Ernest is grinning now. "Can we see her?"

Maggie shakes her head. "We're not allowed to right now. I saw her for a short while but she's under observation because she came early."

Martin is looking around the room. "We're going to have to bring John up when it's okay to see her."

Maggie nods. She looks very happy. A Nurse comes in. She is holding flowers. "Who are those from?"

The Nurse looks at a card. "The message says "CONGRATULATIONS ON YOUR NEW BABY GIRL, FROM DAVID OSWALD!""

Martin looks at Maggie. He has a look very close to a scowl on his face. "Who's David Oswald?"

Maggie looks at the nurse. "Do you remember what he was wearing?"

The Nurse nods. "Yes. He was wearing a suit. It looked quite expensive. I think it was a designer suit."

"What colour was it?"

"It was grey."

Maggie has an unreadable expression on her face. Everyone is looking at her to see what is going on.

"Are you good at describing people?"

CHAPTER SEVEN

1.

Maggie is enjoying her life as a mother. Sheila is standing in Maggie's living room, watching mother and daughter playing. Maggie is happier than she has felt in a long time.

"When are you going back to work?"

Maggie shakes her head. "I can't go back to work. There's nobody to look after Maggie."

"I can look after her. I have to stay at home and look after John anyway."

Maggie looks at her. "That's not fair on you."

Sheila smiles. "It'll bring some life into the house. Anyway, you can't afford this house if you're not working."

Maggie nods and looks at her new daughter. "You're right. When my maternity leave is up I'll get right back to work."

Sheila smiles as the baby plays.

2.

Maggie strides into the classroom and smiles at her class. "Good morning! I've been gone for some time so I have no idea what you're doing at the moment. So turn to page 306 and we'll see what we can do…"

3.

Matthew and Andrew are sitting drinking coffee. Maggie and Lynn walk in. Andrew smiles at them. "Morning ladies!"

"Andrew and I were just about to go to the cafeteria to see if we could find something edible to eat. Would you ladies like to accompany us?"

Lynn shakes her head. "I'm okay."

"I'm starved, but I'll catch up."

"Okay."

Matthew and Andrew walk out of the room and Maggie spins round to Lynn.

"I have to tell you something that has been nagging at my mind since I gave birth to little Maggie."

"You're not looking for a father figure for her already are you?"

Maggie shakes her head. "Christ, no."

"Then what is it?"

"Do you remember that dream man that I told you about?"

Lynn nods.

"He's a real person."

Lynn's eyes widen. "How can he be? He's from a dream."

Maggie shrugs. "I don't know. But he sent me flowers at the Hospital."

Lynn cocks her head to one side. "Did you see him?"

Maggie shakes her head. "I didn't. But the nurse who took the flowers did. And she described him exactly as he was in my dream right down to the grey suit that he was wearing."

Lynn is puzzled. "Did you find out his second name?"

Maggie nods. "Yes, I did. It was Oswald. His full name is David Oswald."

Lynn lets out a gasp of air. "So is he good looking?"

Maggie nods. "Gorgeous!"

"You need to find this guy."

Maggie shakes her head. "Maybe I'm not supposed to."

Lynn laughs at this. "Are you joking? This is the man of your dreams."

Maggie laughs too.

4.

Lynn is putting things into her friend's freezer when Maggie comes in with her baby. Lynn makes faces at little Maggie and the child's face has a toothless smile.

"Maybe you should go to one of those Private Detectives. One of my friends knew a good one in the middle of the city who found her missing brother for her. He'd run away with some satanic cult. Boy, he was really fu…" Lynn looks at little Maggie. "He was really messed up."

Maggie shakes her head. "I've decided not to pursue this David. If I'm destined to meet him then it will happen. Maybe it'll be an accident."

Lynn holds up a tin of chopped tomatoes. "Where do you want me to put these?"

5.

Maggie comes into her parents house with little Maggie. She puts her down on the floor and she starts crawling around. Sheila watches the baby. John is staring into space as usual. Maggie gives a smile to her dad, whose eyes flicker to her.

"Hi Dad. Hi Mum."

"Do you want to stay for dinner?"

Maggie nods. "I'd love that."

Little Maggie is sitting, looking at John. Her eyes blink and she looks at him. John smiles at her - the first time that he has managed a full smile since his stroke. Little Maggie smiles back at him. Sheila and Maggie are happy.

6.

Keith is sitting alone on his bed. He looks out of the window. It is raining hard outside. He picks up a book and tries to read it.

7.

Maggie is walking up the path with little Maggie in a pram. She hears a cough behind her and she turns round. Andrew is walking up the path behind her. "Hello Mum."

Maggie laughs. "I was just passing…"

"You live on the other side of town, Andrew."

"I got lost. Anyway, I saw your house and thought this would be a great time to ask Maggie out to dinner."

"You mean in a date sort of way?"

Andrew shrugs. "If you don't like the sound of that then we could think of it as two people with no social life's wallowing in each other's misery."

Maggie nods. "I'd like that."

Andrew smiles. "Good. How does tomorrow night hit you?"

Maggie nods. "That is, if I can get my Mother to look after little Maggie."

"So it's a date?"

"It's a date."

Andrew walks away backwards and trips up, falling onto his back. Maggie tries to stifle her laugh. He gets up and brushes himself down. "I don't normally do stuff like that. I think my shoes are too tight."

Maggie nods and heads for the front door. "Good night, Andrew!"

"Good night, Maggie!"

8.

Maggie and Andrew talk all through dinner and generally have fun. Andrew pours more red wine. Maggie shakes her head when he puts the bottle to her glass. He looks at her. Maggie shrugs and nods. He fills it three quarters full. The night goes well.

9.

Back at her house, Maggie is drinking a glass of water. Andrew is looking out of the window.

"We're going to regret this in the morning."

Andrew spins round with shock. "What?"

"We're going to regret drinking in the morning. I don't know if I can face first period with a hangover."

Andrew's whole body seems to relax. "Oh."

Maggie looks at her watch. "Thanks for walking me home, Andrew. But it's getting late and I think that you should phone a Taxi."

Andrew nods. "You're right. But I'll go out onto the street and hail one."

"I can phone one."

Andrew raises a hand and shakes his head. "It's okay. I need some air."

Maggie walks Andrew out of the room.

10.

Andrew walks down the path and turns to Maggie. "Do you know what? I think I'd rather walk."

Maggie laughs. "You're mad."

Andrew nods in a really stupid way and walks out of the garden. Maggie watches him go.

11.

Andrew walks through the red light district in the opposite direction from the way that Keith came down on that fateful night. The women are ignoring him because he has the demeanour of someone who is not interested. The prostitute who took Keith home steps out from a shop door. "Are you looking for business?"

Andrew shakes his head. "No thanks! I'm in love."

"Suit yourself."

12.

Maggie comes into her mother and father's Living room. Little Maggie is getting older now. Maggie picks her up and kisses her. "Soon you'll be talking honey and you and I can stay up all night and have the greatest conversations."

Sheila hugs her daughter. John is the same as he always is.

13.

At Lynn's place, she and Matthew are having a drink. Lynn smiles. "Don't you think that Maggie is looking great?"

Matthew nods. "It makes me wonder why I'm wasting my time with you."

Lynn punches him in the arm. "You Bastard!"

They both laugh. "Andrew's looks good as well. Since he started taking her out for meals and stuff."

"Do you think that the two of them will get together?"

Matthew shrugs. "They've not even kissed yet as far as I can tell. I think the main question we should be asking is, is my best friend gay?"

Lynn drains her glass. "I don't think that Maggie's looking for anything right now."

"That's a shame. I think that they would make a great couple."

"Do you want another?"

14.

Maggie is sitting, reading. Little Maggie is playing when the doorbell goes.

15.

Martin is standing at the door. He is dressed in his Police uniform. Maggie opens the door and smiles at him. "I was just passing…" He tells her.

"I get a lot of that."

16.

Martin sits down.

"Do you want a cup of coffee?"

Martin shakes his head. "A glass of water would be nice."

Maggie nods. She leaves the room and Martin looks at little Maggie. "Hello there!"

Little Maggie starts to cry and Martin sits back in his chair. Maggie comes back in with the water and laughs. Little Maggie is still in tears.

"You don't really have a good effect on kids, Martin, do you?"

He gives her a smile and takes the water off of her. Maggie picks up her baby and tries to console her. "I'm usually so good with kids."

Maggie smiles.

"There was a reason for me coming round."

"Yeah?"

"Keith's in jail."

"What?"

17.

Maggie is sitting on the couch. She has little Maggie in her arms. Lynn is sitting across from her.

"Apparently he went to the red light district and attacked a prostitute for no reason."

"Jesus!"

Maggie nods. "I know. The Police got there before he was able to get to her. He was drunk. The Police are keeping him over the weekend."

"Are you going to go and see him?"

Maggie shakes her head. "Hell, no!"

"Day Bid." Little Maggie says.

Lynn looks at the baby. "She spoke!"

CHAPTER EIGHT

1.

Maggie is sitting in her parents living room with her baby in her arms and Sheila is looking at her.

"And do you know what her first words were?"

Sheila shakes her head.

"Day Bid. We think she was trying to say David." Maggie laughs. "Is that not freaky? I keep hearing that name."

Sheila smiles. "That was your first word."

Maggie stops laughing and looks serious. "What do you mean?"

Sheila nods. "Your uncle David lived with us for a while when his wife threw him out for…" Sheila stops to think. "I think it was something like the fourth or fifth time. Anyway he was around you a lot and you said Day bid before you even said Mum or Dad."

The two of them sit there in silence for a while.

2.

Young Maggie is a lot older now and she is walking. Maggie and Andrew are drinking coffee together in the Kitchen. He looks at the child. "So what are you doing tonight?"

Andrew shakes his head. "I was thinking of going to the cinema. Want to come with me?"

Maggie shakes her head. "I can't. It's a bit late notice for my mum to look after Maggie."

Young Maggie comes over with a yellow Lego brick and hands it to Andrew. "That yours."

She giggles uncontrollably and Andrew smiles at her. "I'm going put this in my pocket."

"No! It's mine."

She snatches it back.

3.

Andrew steps outside and Keith is standing there. Maggie looks at him. "What are you doing here?"

"Is this the new boyfriend?"

Andrew is standing there, not sure what to do.

"He's just a friend."

Just a friend, Andrew thinks, a little depressed.

"Good."

"And what would it matter to my ex husband if he was my boyfriend?"

Andrew is nervous. Keith looks at him.

"What would you be able to say if I told you that he and I had just fucked for an hour on the carpet?"

Keith looks at her. "I didn't come for a fight."

"And what did you come for? Did you forget something?"

"Yes, I forgot something. I forgot what you looked like and I forgot how much I loved you."

"Well I forget ever loving you. Get the hell away from this house."

"I'd best be going," Andrew says to nobody in particular.

"I'll see you tomorrow, Andrew. Enjoy the Cinema tonight."

"Yeah, Andrew. Enjoy the Cinema tonight."

"I will, Keith. Thanks."

Maggie smiles as Andrew walks away. Keith looks at her. "Can I come in?"

Maggie shakes her head. "I think you should just go. You ruined your chances of getting back with me when you filed for divorce. Do you know that I went into labour while I read your fucking letter?"

Keith looks at her for a second and walks away.

4.

Andrew is walking down the street when Keith catches up with him. His car is parked round the corner from Maggie's House.

"Hey."

Andrew turns round.

"Keep away from my wife."

"You mean ex wife?"

Keith looks angry. "Keep the fuck away from her, okay."

Andrew shakes his head. Keith punches Andrew and he falls back onto the bonnet of his car. Keith starts walking away. He touches his cheek and winces. He strides after Keith and taps him on the shoulder. Keith turns round. "Want some more?"

Keith grabs him and throws him to the ground. He kicks him in the ribs. Andrew screams in pain. Keith stands over him and Andrew struggles to get up. Keith watches him. Andrew looks at him for a second and laughs. He then punches Keith squarely between the eyes. His nose explodes in a puff of blood and he falls on his back. Andrew gets into his car and drives away. Keith lies there, groaning.

5.

Keith pushes the door to his flat open and steps inside. His nose is still bloodied. "Hello?"

A figure with a mask on comes running out of the darkness. Keith falls onto his back and the figure is on top of him, punching at him.

6.

Maggie is watching her daughter play with Lego. There is a knock at the door and she gets up to answer.

7.

Ernest and Martin are standing there with a badly bruised Keith. He smiles at her and she sees that a few of his teeth are missing.

"Can we come in, Maggie?"

Maggie nods.

8.

They are all sitting together. Keith is wincing in pain.

"What the hell happened?"

Young Maggie comes up with a selection of bricks. She hands a yellow one to Ernest, who takes it from her and smiles.

"Honey, you have to believe everything that I'm going tell you."

Maggie nods.

Young Maggie is watching Ernest as he twists the Lego brick round in circles with his fingers. He keeps looking at her.

"Your boyfriend punched me last night."

"He is not my boyfriend. He is just a friend."

Keith waves it off. "I started it. I have to admit. Looking back, I was being a dick as usual."

Maggie nods. "Punching you is not going to do that to your face. And anyway, he phoned me when he got home to apologise to me for doing it."

Keith shakes his head. "It doesn't end there."

Maggie sits forward in her chair. "I kind of guessed that."

"I got attacked last night when I got into the house. It was a guy in a mask."

9.

The Masked man punches Maggie in the face and she falls to the ground.

10.

Keith is shaking as he talks. Maggie has a tear forming in her eye. "He grabbed me and started kicking me and punching me. He kicked me to the ground. He kept punching and kicking. I begged him for mercy. He said…"

11.

The Masked Man grabs Keith by the throat. "I didn't beeping stop when your wife asked me to. I beeped her brains out in an alley. Why should I stop when you ask?"

Keith has blood coming from his mouth. The Masked Man laughs. "She was my property the moment I did that to her. You've lost her. She's mine now. And if you go near my bitch again I'll cut your beeping throat."

12.

Maggie is shaking. Keith turns to Martin and Ernest. "Obviously he didn't say beeping. I'm just trying to protect the kid's ears."

Martin nods. Ernest hands the Lego back to young Maggie, as she won't leave him alone.

"He was trying to hide his voice but every time I try to hear it now, I hear you friend."

Maggie shakes her head. "You think that Andrew kicked the hell out of you?"

She stands up. "You think that Andrew raped me?"

Keith is cowering, as he has never seen Maggie so angry before.

"I have never heard such bullshit in my life before. Get the hell out of my house."

Keith nods. Martin stands up. "We need to follow this up, Maggie. Can you give me Andrew's address?"

Maggie shakes her head. "No, I can't."

"I thought you would want to. I can go to the school for it and if I have to do that then they will ask questions."

Maggie shoots a look at Keith. "He's just using this to make me miserable. He can't have me so he's trying to ruin my life."

"I wouldn't do that, honey."

Maggie stands to him face to face. Young Maggie is standing beside Martin. He is watching, worried. Young Maggie hands him the Lego brick, which he takes. She has another one in her hand. "Why don't you fuck off and do something that you're good at… Like beating up prostitutes. And don't call me honey."

Martin gives a small cough. "Maggie, please just give us Andrew's address and we can be gone."

Maggie looks right into Keith's eyes. "I never ever want to see you at this house again. Is that clear?"

Keith nods slowly.

"Say it!"

"It's clear."

Maggie's face changes and she turns to Martin and Ernest.

"Andrew stays at 315 Sheridan Drive."

Ernest smiles. "We'll get all of this cleared up and then you can continue with your life."

A Lego Brick hurtles out of nowhere and hits Ernest on this side of the head. He blinks a couple of times but does not seem to notice.

13.

Ernest walks up to Andrew's door with another Policeman. He knocks on the door and waits for a second. Andrew answers. He looks surprised to see the Police standing there. "Can I help you?"

Ernest nods. "Are you Mr. Andrew Dodd?"

Andrew nods. "Could you accompany us down to the station sir? We have a couple of questions we would like to ask you?"

"Is this about Keith?"

14.

Ernest and Martin are sitting in front of Andrew, who looks tired and annoyed. "I am telling you that I did not go back to Keith's house last night."

"And you did not rape his wife?"

Andrew looks at him. "Ex Wife!"

"Answer the question Mr. Dodd."

"No, I did not rape her. Maggie is a friend."

Martin smiles and sits back in his chair. "Maggie is a friend. So you have no sexual feelings for her whatsoever."

Andrew looks astonished. "What the hell does that have to do with anything?"

"Let me see. Could it be because I'm trying to establish whether or not you are capable of raping her because you know you could never have her?"

Andrew lets out an astonished gasp. "Are you for real? This isn't "The Bill". Real Policemen do not talk like that."

Martin is getting annoyed. "Look son, I don't think you realise how much trouble you are in."

"I did not attack Keith last night and I did not rape Maggie!"

"Do you have an alibi?"

Andrew nods. "I have an alibi for when Maggie was raped. So if the rapist attacked Keith then it follows that I could not have done that either."

Martin looks annoyed.

"So where were you when Maggie was being raped?" Ernest asks.

15.

Andrew is sitting in the front of thc Taxi, beside the Taxi Driver. Lynn and Matthew are in the back, kissing each other all over. The driver keeps looking in the mirror at them and he has a look of discomfort on his face. But he does not seem to be that bothered - he sees it every week. Andrew looks quite embarrassed. Matthew stops kissing Lynn and looks at Andrew.

"Are you coming back to my house?"

Lynn looks a bit annoyed by this. Andrew shakes his head. "No thanks, mate. I'll just go home."

"Just come back to mine. You can crash out somewhere."

"He doesn't want to go, Matthew. Let him do what he wants."

Matthew starts tapping Andrew on the shoulder. "Andrew, mate!"

"What?"

Matthew gets annoyed. "Andrew, mate!"

"I said what?"

"I didn't hear you."

There is silence for a moment. "Well, what?"

"Are you coming back to my house?"

Andrew lets out an annoyed sigh.

16.

Matthew and Lynn are kissing again whilst dancing to 70's music and Andrew is sitting with a glass of water in his hand. He takes a loud sip and Matthew stops. "We're ignoring Andy here."

Matthew comes right up to Andrew's face and kisses him square on the lips. "You're my best fucking pal."

"You're my best fucking pal too."

"Fucking Brilliant."

"Do you have any more vodka, Matt?" Lynn asks.

Matthew spins round. "Don't call me Matt. My brother used to call me fat Matt. I used to hate it."

"You were never fat!" Lynn says.

"I fucking was."

Andrew looks at his watch. It says 5:13. He lets out another sigh. "I should be going."

"You just got here!" Matthew tells him.

"It's nearly quarter past five. I've been here for ages."

Matthew looks confused. "Oh."

"You go home, Andrew and we'll see you on Monday."

Andrew nods and gets up. He is quite drunk too although he is the most sober of the group. He hugs Lynn. "I hope you two are happy together."

Matthew nods. "If I can get it up."

He laughs with a drunken ferocity. Andrew walks slowly to the door and stops, turning round. "I hope you two are happy together."

Matthew stops laughing and looks at him. "If I can get it up."

He starts laughing again and Lynn rolls her eyes.

17.

Andrew looks at Martin and Ernest calmly. "I was at a friend's house. And I have two witnesses."

CHAPTER NINE

1.

Maggie is sitting in her chair. Young Maggie is playing with a toy next to her. She is still in a state of shock about the whole day so far. There is a knock at the door.

2.

Andrew is standing there. He looks tired. "It wasn't me, Maggie. I swear to you."

Maggie nods. "Do you want to come in for a cup of coffee?"

Andrew shakes his head. "I'd better not. I'll wait until all of this calms down."

Maggie nods again and Andrew starts walking from the house.

3.

Time continues on its course and Young Maggie is six. She walks over to her mother in her school uniform.

"Hi, honey."

Young Maggie positively beams with joy at her mother. "Hi, Mum. Are you still going to dinner with Andrew tonight?"

Maggie shrugs. "I don't know."

"I want to stay at Auntie Lynn and Uncle Matt's house tonight."

Maggie smiles. "Okay then. I suppose I'll go out to dinner with Andrew. But just for you."

Young Maggie laughs.

4.

Matthew walks into the room with Young Maggie. Lynn walks in from the Kitchen. There is a piano in the corner with Matthew and Lynn's wedding picture on top. Young Maggie looks at it.

"When did you get that?"

"My Dad left it to me in his will."

Young Maggie has a look of child like wonder on her face. "I've been learning. My teacher says I have a natural talent."

"I've never been able to play. What can you play?"

"I am perfecting Fur Elise right now

"How does that go?"

"It's Beethoven," says Matthew. "And I think it's quite difficult for someone your age."

"My teacher says I have a natural talent."

Matthew nods and smiles. "Play it for us."

Young Maggie runs over to the Piano with a squeak of delight. She starts to play and she is good. The couple almost find it hard to believe that Young Maggie is playing it. Lynn is shocked. Matthew claps loudly when she finishes. "That was fu…"

Lynn coughs and looks at him. He stops.

"That was excellent."

"Thanks."

5.

Maggie is smiling as she eats in the restaurant. Andrew takes sip of wine. "So, how is Maggie getting on at school?"

Maggie nods. "She's very bright. She's good at all the subjects I was good at. Her spelling is tremendous. She is having a little trouble with her multiplication tables but it will come to her sooner or later. She's only young."

Andrew nods.

"So, David, do you want to go to the cinema tomorrow? There's a great film on in…"

She realises that Andrew is looking at her.

"What?"

"You called me David."

Maggie looks at him. "I did?"

Andrew nods. "You did."

She lets out a little laugh.

"So, who's David? Some guy that you've got your eye on?"

Maggie laughs. "You know that I'm not interested in relationships. I just enjoy going out with friends."

Andrew nods. "Yeah, I know."

There is silence for a moment and Maggie takes a small sip of her wine.

"So who is David then?"

"I don't know. I've not thought about him for ages."

"An old friend?"

Maggie laughs. "In a manner of speaking!"

Andrew looks confused.

"Look, do you promise that you won't laugh?"

Andrew raises a hand. "I swear."

"I've never met him. He's a dream man."

"A dream man?"

"I got physical proof after Maggie was born that he existed. But I've only ever seen him in my dreams."

Andrew is confused.

"I dream of him in times of crisis. But I haven't thought of him for so long. He was the reason that I wasn't so traumatised by my rape. He helped me through it. I don't even remember anything about the sex thanks to him."

Andrew looks uncomfortable.

"I think he's my Guardian Angel."

Andrew takes a bite out of a piece of bread and watches her as he swallows it down.

"I know that it sounds crazy."

Andrew smiles. "Not at all! It sounds great. I wish I had a Guardian Angel."

Maggie looks embarrassed. "I actually have had a bit of a crush on him since I started dreaming about him."

Andrew's face falls. "How long have you dreamt of him."

Maggie laughs. "That's the thing. After he helped me through the rape, I realised that he had been in my dreams for my whole life, but I had forgotten them. They started to come back in fragments and now I think my earliest memory of him was when I was six."

"You were six?"

Maggie nods.

"And you have a crush on him?"

Maggie nods. "Just a little."

"Do you want dessert?"

6.

Maggie walks into the room with Lynn and sees Matthew playing with Young Maggie.

"How was she?"

Lynne laughs. "She's great. It's like she looks after us instead of vice versa."

"Mum says that too."

"How is your dad?"

Maggie shakes her head. "My Mum puts on a brave face but seven years of it is wearing her down."

Matthew and Young Maggie come over. "You didn't tell us you had a prodigy for a daughter."

Maggie looks confused.

"She played the Piano for us. Her teacher taught her well. Who was it?"

Maggie looks at young Maggie, who has a smile on her face.

"Nobody has taught her to play the Piano."

Matthew looks confused.

"She played Fur Elise for us."

Maggie takes a step back, as if she is expecting young Maggie to strike her. She looks pale.

"What is it?" Lynn asks

"She has never had a Piano lesson in her life."

"She told us she was being taught. And the played in front of us!"

"That was the first piece of music I learnt. I was six. And I always made a mistake close to the beginning."

Young Maggie nods.

"I bet you made the same mistake, didn't you?"

Matthew looks confused. "What's going on?"

Maggie shakes her head. "Nothing! I'm tired. Are you ready to come home, honey?"

Young Maggie nods and takes her Mother's hand. They walk out of the Living Room together and Lynn and Matthew exchange confused looks.

7.

Maggie is looking at her Daughter. "What is going on?"

Young Maggie shakes her head. "I know things…"

"What things do you know?"

"Things about you!"

"You have the same school abilities as me, you were born prematurely like me, and you play the piano like me. And the first word you say was the first word that I uttered when I was your age."

Young Maggie nods.

"What the hell is going on?"

Young Maggie begins to cry. "I'm scared."

"So am I, honey."

The two of them hug.

"David will lead us on the path."

Maggie breaks the hug and looks at her. "What did you say?"

8.

Maggie and Young Maggie are walking around, buying groceries. Young Maggie picks things off of the shelf that her mother wants without asking. Martin is walking around as well, looking for food. The two groups are unaware of one another. The miss each other by seconds as Martin goes round a different corner. But they keep going around one another and after a short while there is the inevitable meeting between the two of them. Young Maggie looks up at him.

"Hi ladies!" He says

"Hi, Martin."

"I saw your dad the other day..."

His mobile phone starts ringing. "I'm sorry." He answers it. "Yes? He did what? Is Ernest not around? Oh, yeah, I forgot about that. Okay, I'll be there as soon as possible. Don't panic."

Martin switches the phone off. "There is an emergency back at the station. I have to run. See you both later."

He moves off.

"Bye, Martin!"

"Bye, daddy!" Young Maggie says.

Martin freezes for a second but continues. Maggie looks down at her daughter with a questioning look. Young Maggie merely nods.

CHAPTER TEN

1.

It is the night of the party again and Maggie is standing beside the old woman when Martin walks over to her. "Won't you dance with me Maggie?"

Maggie gives a nervous smile. "I can't really dance to this kind of music, Martin!"

Martin starts dancing strangely in front of her. "Come on, it'll be fun."

Maggie shakes her head. "I'm sorry."

Martin nods. "It's okay. But I want a dance later."

Martin shuffles away with his bizarre dance. "Won't somebody dance with me?"

The phrase seems to echo into infinity…

2.

Martin is lying awake, sweating all over, his wife fast asleep beside him. He can still hear his own voice echoing in his ears as he looks at the ceiling. Slowly, a smile appears on his face.

3.

Martin is standing at the bar watching the group of teachers drinking. Maggie does not look to be enjoying herself. He watches Lynn turn to Maggie. She says something and Maggie smiles, saying something back to her. The drinking continues. Matthew staggers over to the dance floor. He dances on his own for a few moments, as the others laugh at him. Lynn turns to Maggie and says something to her. Martin licks his lips as he watches what is going on. Maggie shakes her head. Lynn gets up and staggers over to Matthew. The two of them dance drunkenly. Another Teacher, Andrew Dodd, slides over to Maggie. This makes Martin look angry. They start talking to one another. Andrew laughs sharply. Maggie winces at the sound of it. He points at Maggie and Matthew. Martin does not like what he is seeing and knocks back the rest of his drink. Maggie watches as the two of them dance closely. The two people on the dance floor kiss and Martin turns to the barman. "Can I have another pint?"

The Barman nods.

4.

Maggie is walking along the alley when she hears a noise behind her. She spins round. Martin is standing there. Maggie looks scared, and she sobers up instantly. "I don't have much money. But you can take it."

"I don't want your fucking money."

Maggie takes a step back. "I'll scream."

As fast as lightning, Martin punches her in the face and she falls to the ground. Her nose is dripping blood and she looks up at him. He is on top of her in a second, ripping at her clothes. He puts his hand over her mouth and stifles her screams. Maggie's eyes are open wide. They are darting from left to right. Her skirt is lifted up and her underwear is ripped from her.

5.

Martin is sitting at his desk in a Police Uniform. David Oswald is standing in front of him with his Grey Suit. He laughs. "So that's how you remember it, Martin?"

Martin looks at him. "Who the fuck are you?"

David looks at him. "There is no need for that language."

Martin is thrown from his chair. He hits off of the wall behind him. He gets up and looks at David. He is scared. "Who are you?"

"I am more than you can imagine. I have been before you before."

Martin picks up his chair and puts it back under his desk. He tries to look dignified.

"You won't remember. Only the gifted do. You are not gifted."

Martin laughs. "Get out of my office."

David looks around. "You see your office? That must be the place where you feel most comfortable."

"Get out!"

David grabs Martin by the throat and puts him against the wall again. "You never answered my question. Do you remember it that way?"

Martin looks at him. "What are you talking about?"

"The night you raped Maggie? Do you remember walking up to her with your true face?"

Martin shakes his head. "I don't know what the fuck you are talking about."

Blue sparks come from the hand that David is not holding Martin's throat with. "I told you not to use that kind of language and you don't really want to see me angry. Do you, Martin?"

Martin doesn't say anything.

"I'm going to ask you again. Do you remember showing your true face to Maggie?"

"One of my men will be here in a minute and we'll see who the big man is then."

David laughs. "You're in bed right now beside your wife. You're not really in your office. Now answer me, Martin."

The door opens and a Policeman walks in. Martin laughs. "Oh, really."

"Really!"

Martin looks at the Policeman again and it is John. He smiles at Martin. "Hello, Martin!"

Martin screams.

"Did you show my daughter your face when you raped her?"

Martin nods. "Yeah, she saw it. I flaunted it."

John and David laugh.

"Bullshit. You never had the guts."

Martin looks at David. "He swore. Zap him."

David shakes his head. "I like John."

Martin looks at John again. He has the mask on his head that Martin used when he was raping Maggie.

"Is this your true face, Martin? Because this is what you showed my daughter."

"I never wore a mask. I didn't need one. Your daughter wanted me. She hid it as a rape to keep Keith happy."

John takes the mask off and throws it to the ground. "You have sown the seeds of your own end. You do realise that? I only wish that I could be around to see the end."

Martin is dropped to the ground. David walks over to John.

"Why should I listen to anything you have to say, you vegetable?"

"You were my best friend, Martin. I told you everything. I even told you about the time I cheated on my wife one night and regretted it for seven years. But there was a sickness inside you. I remember when you used to play with Maggie when she was four. Did you want to fuck her then?"

Martin runs at John and is thrown back against the wall by an invisible force. He sneers at John. "You're damned right I wanted to fuck her then. And I wanted to do it in front of you and your wife. That would have been a story to tell the grandkids, huh? Just remember that I'm the father of that Bastard kid. And when I get a chance, I'll fuck her too. I'll fuck them all."

Martin's nose starts to bleed and he gasps for breath. He falls forward.

6.

Martin's eyes pop open and he feels he can't breathe. There is blood pouring out of his nose.

7.

Sheila walks into the living room. John is sitting in front of the television. Martin walks in, too.

"Martin's here to see you."

Martin waves. "Hi John."

"Where is Ernest?"

Martin smiles. "He's busy right now. So I thought I would say hi for both of us."

Sheila smiles.

"Can I speak to John alone for a minute?" He tries to be as sincere as he can. "I just know that he can hear me."

Sheila nods. "I'll just go and make a cup of coffee."

She steps out of the room and Martin walks over to John. He crouches down in front of him. "Hey John, how is it going?"

John does not move.

"I know you can hear me. And I know that guy in the grey suit is real as well. But in this world you are nothing. And if you are going to punish me in the other realm well I am going to do the same to you here."

He kisses John on the lips. "I thought that you should be the first one to know. I am going to go round to Maggie's house some time this week and fuck her brains out again. Then maybe young Maggie can get some. She has to learn about the birds and the bees sooner or later. Then I might just blow both their fucking heads off. Then your wife can read about it in the newspaper. And then I'll come by here and give her my condolences." He takes one of John's hands in his. "And do you know what I'm going to do then?"

Martin puts his nose against John's.

"I'm going to take Sheila and I'm going to rape her on that sofa over there…"

He points in the general direction of the sofa. "I'm going to make sure that you get a ringside seat and watch as I fuck her brains out. Then I'm going to kill her too. And do you know what I'm going to do to you?"

Martin waits for an answer that doesn't come.

"I'm going to do absolutely nothing!"

He starts laughing. "I am going to let you sit there and see that image before your eyes, along with the knowledge of what I have done, for the rest of your piss miserable life. And I'll sit back with your job and think about getting in touch with Ernest's relatives. Maybe his daughter will dance with me."

Martin looks sad. "She wouldn't dance with me. It was the straw that broke the camel's back. If she had danced with me I could have imagined our bodies together and maybe just masturbated. But no, I had to experience the real thing."

Sheila comes back into the room with two cups of tea and biscuits. "Are you two boys done?"

Martin nods. "Oh yes."

His eyes light up.

"Are those chocolate ginger nuts?"

8.

Maggie is sitting in her room, wiping tears from her eyes. Young Maggie is sitting, playing.

"What are you?"

Young Maggie blinks at her and smiles. "What do you think I am?"

Maggie shakes her head. "I don't know."

Young Maggie raises her right arm. Maggie finds herself raising hers at the same time. Young Maggie laughs, but not maliciously. She drops her hand and Maggie's falls too. "I love you Mum. Never forget that."

Maggie nods and smiles. "I love you too."

There is a knock at the door. Maggie gets up.

9.

Maggie answers the door and Lynn is standing there. "I was worried when you phoned in sick today."

Maggie shakes her head. "I had a bad day yesterday."

Lynn looks at her. "What is it?"

Maggie starts crying. "I think I know who raped me, Lynn."

10.

Maggie has calmed down by now. She and Lynn are drinking coffee.

"So what are you going to do?"

Maggie shrugs. "I can't go to the Police."

"Why the hell not?"

"He's a cop for Christ's sake. They look after their own."

"Bullshit."

Young Maggie is watching them attentively.

"I'd just be scared."

"There must be someone there who you could trust."

Maggie nods. "There is someone. My dad's other friend, Ernest Robson."

Lynn smiles. "Well, go to him, then."

Maggie shakes her head. "He has been a friend of Martin's for as long as my dad has. I can't spring this on him."

Lynn lets out an annoyed gasp. "Then what are you going to do, then?"

"Remember years ago, you were going to give me the name of a Private Investigator?"

Lynn nods.

"Can you get it for me now?"

Lynn nods.

11.

Maggie and Young Maggie walk towards a lovely building. She double-checks the address before stepping inside.

12.

The office is empty except for one woman sitting at a desk.

"Good morning, how can I help?"

Maggie smiles. "Sorry, I was expecting a man…"

Alice smiles. "I'll just buzz him through."

She picks up a phone. "Hi. There's a woman here to see you."

She listens intently. "Is your name Maggie Hooper?"

Maggie is surprised by the question.

"Yes."

"Go right in. He's expecting you."

Maggie nods and goes in with young Maggie.

13.

Maggie and her daughter step inside and she lets out a small gasp as she sees that it is David Oswald, sporting his grey suit, who is standing in front of her.

"Hi Maggie. My name is David Oswald, but I think that you know that."

He looks at young Maggie. "And this must be your daughter?"

He smiles at Maggie.

"She looks just like you."

CHAPTER ELEVEN

1.

Maggie is still rooted to the spot as David is crouched down, smiling at Young Maggie.

"I was wondering when you would give your mother a clue about the man that she has been looking for."

Young Maggie gives a small child like giggle. David stands up and offers his hand out for Maggie to shake it. She does but cannot seem to bring out any words.

"There is a lot to be done."

Maggie nods.

"Now that you know who raped you we have to bring him to justice as swiftly as possible."

Maggie nods again. It seems that this is all she is capable of at the moment.

"First things first…"

Maggie seems to regain her voice and shakes her head. "Wait a minute. Martin is a Policeman. He will have found hundreds of ways to cover up what he has done by now. He's had about seven years. There is no way that we are ever going to prove that he was near me when I was raped."

David nods sombrely. "You are correct."

"I know that I am correct. I have thought about not much else."

Young Maggie is looking around the room.

"Then why did you come here? Oh and by the way this has not been a Private Investigator's for some time. We're a software company."

"You are?" Maggie asks. Then, "I don't know why I came. It just felt like the right thing to do. Like it was supposed to happen."

David nods sympathetically and puts a hand on her shoulder. She gives a little shiver and is not sure if it is excitement or fear.

"I can tell you now that if you continue down this road with me it will lead to your attacker being brought to justice. Martin will pay for what he has done."

Maggie nods and smiles. A tear appears at the corner of her left eye.

"I believe you."

David looks sad. "But there will be losses. The loss to you will be great."

"What do you mean?"

"This situation is too far down the road for no losses to be felt."

"What do you mean?"

"You can walk away right now and Martin will never be brought to Justice. But he knows that you know now and I think he may try to silence you."

Maggie stands and thinks about this for a moment. "So I can't walk away at all?"

David shrugs. "You can. But I don't know if it will work. Contrary to popular belief, I don't know everything."

Young Maggie stands beside David. "You can't walk away mum. No matter what happens."

Maggie looks at the two of them. "But what can I do? I can't go to the Police."

David looks at Young Maggie. "Could you go outside to Alice and tell her that I said you were to look after her for a couple of minutes?"

Young Maggie nods and skips happily out of the room. He walks to a cupboard and takes a key out of his pocket. Maggie watches him.

"What are you doing?"

David opens the cupboard and takes something out of it. He walks over to Maggie and presents her with a gun.

"What the hell is this for?"

David does not look happy about it. "If the Police can do nothing then we are going to have to take matters into our own hands."

Maggie shakes her head. "I can't use a gun."

David smiles. "It will come to you."

"But I don't think I could shoot someone in cold blood."

"Then only shoot at him if he comes to get you."

Maggie backs off. "I'm sorry, but I can't do this."

"You have to. You have to do this for the sake of your father."

Maggie stops.

"Your dad is powerless for the most part in this realm to bring Martin to justice. But there are other realms. Killing Martin will put him in reach of your father's wrath for the rest of time and then we justice will be brought about. The punishment of Martin does not end when you pull that trigger. It just begins."

Maggie takes the gun from him and looks at it. "I don't know if I can do this."

"Like I said, it will come to you."

2.

Maggie is sitting in her house with the gun in her hand. She hears a noise and spins round to look to see who is there. It is Andrew. "I just let myself in…"

He sees the gun.

"Jesus, Maggie, where did you get that?"

Maggie puts her finger to her lips. "Maggie is upstairs asleep."

"What are you doing with a gun?"

"Sit down, Andrew."

Andrew sits down on the couch but not too close to her.

"I know who raped me."

"What? Who?"

He looks angered by this.

"It was Martin."

"Who the hell is Martin?"

"You know? The Policeman who arrested you for doing it!"

Andrew looks confused for a second. "You mean the bald one?"

Maggie shakes her head. "No. The other one!"

Andrew takes a few moments for this to sink in and his eyes widen. "And you're going to shoot him."

Maggie scowls. "I told you to keep quiet."

Andrew looks sorry. "But can't you go to the Police?"

"I'm fed up with people giving me that option. He is the Police. It's not an option."

"Neither is shooting him. You could go to jail for a long time."

Maggie nods. "He needs to be punished."

"This is not the way."

Maggie is tearful and angry. "Do you think that I haven't thought about all of this? I am only considering it after a lot of thought."

"Who put the idea into your head in the first place?"

Maggie puts the gun on the table and looks at him.

"Who was it?"

"Do you remember that guy that I told you about?"

"What guy?"

"The dream guy! David Oswald!"

Andrew nods.

"It was David."

"So some guy tells you in a dream that you should shoot a man that may be perfectly innocent and you consider doing it?"

"It was Maggie that told me that Martin was the rapist, not David."

Andrew cocks his head to one side and looks at her.

"Your daughter told you that she knows who raped you despite the fact that she wasn't even born at the time and you believe her?"

Maggie nods. "You can't even begin to understand this Andrew."

"Damn right I can't. Then based on this revelation, you have a dream and in it you are told that the best thing to do is to shoot him?"

Maggie shakes her head. "It wasn't a dream. Do you remember that I told you I had proof that he existed in reality as well as in my dreams?"

Andrew nods. He does not like where this conversation is going.

"I met him. I met David Oswald."

Andrew does not seem to register this for a moment and then his eyes widen. "What?"

"I met David Oswald."

"Where?"

"He owns a Software company on Martell Street."

Andrew stops to think for a moment and puts a hand on Maggie's shoulder.

"You don't know this man. You shouldn't just listen to what he tells you."

Maggie is confused. "But I have spoken to him in my dreams."

"Just because you've dreamt of someone doesn't mean that you know what he is like. I don't pretend to know what is going on here. But I am going to go and see this David Oswald."

Maggie shakes her head. "You can't."

"Oh yes I can. What are you going to do? Shoot me?"

Maggie does not know what to say to this. Andrew senses finality, as if the two of them will not meet again before this is over. There is silence and Andrew can see in his eyes he has really hurt her and just how much she loves him. Just then, Andrew moves over and kisses Maggie lightly on the lips. Her eyes close as if she is expecting more of a kiss. But he moves back after the light brushing of their lips and smiles.

"Maggie, I love you."

He stands up and walks towards the door. He turns back to her. She has not moved but her eyes are now open.

"Promise me you will think about whether or not you want to kill this man."

Maggie nods. "I promise, Andrew."

Andrew smiles. "I'll be back soon."

He walks out of the room and Maggie looks at the gun on the table.

3.

It is beginning to darken outside and Young Maggie watches Andrew walk out to his car. She smiles and feels a tear running down her cheek. "She loves you too, Andrew. She just didn't realise it until she felt your kiss."

She walks away from the window and towards the door.

4.

Maggie is sitting, staring still at the gun. Young Maggie walks in to the room and Maggie quickly hides it under a newspaper that is lying beside it. "You should have called me down. I haven't seen uncle Andrew in ages."

"I'm sorry. We were having a serious talk."

"I see."

"Maggie, what would you think if Andrew became more than an uncle?"

Young Maggie giggles. "Do you mean like a Dad?"

"Yes. Not quite, but more that sort of role."

"I've never had a real dad before."

"It would be nice, wouldn't it?"

Young Maggie looks sad. "Yes, it would be nice."

"What's wrong?"

"Nothing!"

She suddenly smiles. "Did he kiss you?"

Maggie puts on a stern look. "I think you already know the answer to that one, madam."

Young Maggie giggles. "Yes, I do."

"How do you do it?"

Young Maggie smiles and taps her nose. "You know deep down."

The two of them smile at one another and neither notice that it is darker still out of the window and that Martin is looking in at them.

CHAPTER TWELVE

1.

David is drinking a cup of coffee and talking to the only other employee still in the building – Alice.

"I need to head off soon David. Chris has been complaining about overtime again."

"There's a surprise."

The door opens and Andrew walks in.

"Hi, could you come back tomorrow? The office has closed for the evening."

David looks at Andrew. "It's okay Alice. Good evening Andrew!"

"You must be David Oswald."

David nods and extends the hand that is not holding a cup of coffee out to Andrew. He takes it before he can even think not to.

"It's a pleasure to finally meet you."

He looks to Alice. "I have to speak to Andrew for a little while."

"So should I go?"

"Yes off you go. Have a good night."

Alice nods. David walks towards his office. "Come in, Andrew."

Andrew nods and follows him in quickly. Alice shakes her head and smiles as she goes to get her jacket.

2.

David walks to his desk and put his coffee down. He sits on his chair and gestures to the other one. "Would you like to sit down?"

Andrew shakes his head. "I'll stand."

"It's a bit of a cliché but it's your choice."

"You gave my friend a gun."

David nods. "Yes. She'll need it."

"She should go to the Police."

David shakes his head. "This is beyond your comprehension, Mr. Dodd. Me, I do things like this for a living. I know that this is for the best."

"How can you know that?"

"Are you still scared of the monster, Andrew?"

Andrew looks annoyed. "What the hell are you talking about?"

"You used to sleep with your bedroom door open. There was a chair in the hall and your father used to leave his jacket and hat on it. Due to the shadows in the middle of the night, you used to wake up and stiffen with fright at the sight. You were convinced it was a monster. Even when you saw what it was in the cold light of day, you would be just as scared the next night, yet too fascinated to ever sleep with the door closed."

Andrew cannot help but smile. "How do you know all this?"

"Because of who I am."

"Who are you?"

"Suffice to say Maggie needs that gun."

3.

Maggie and Young Maggie are sitting in the Living room when there is an almighty bang. Maggie takes a sharp intake of breath and dives for the newspaper. Martin walks into the Living Room and smiles. "Hi Maggie. Did you miss me?"

Young Maggie looks at him. "You are going to die."

Martin laughs and takes a switchblade out of his pocket. He pushes a switch and it appears, lethal looking. "On the contrary…"

He rushes at Maggie, who is scrabbling for the gun and kicks her in the stomach. Young Maggie sits and watches. The gun falls to the floor but Martin does not seem to see it.

"Are you ready, Maggie? Are you ready to get fucked again?"

Maggie is looking at him with terrified eyes. Young Maggie dives for him and he slaps her away. Young Maggie strikes a wall and crumples into an unconscious heap. Maggie screams and Martin punches her.

4.

Andrew is looking out of the window. "So when do you think that Martin will try anything?"

"It will probably be soon. He does not want to risk Maggie telling anyone."

"We can stop him. Maggie doesn't need to be a part of this."

"She started down this road when she decided to have her… child. She had a choice then. She chose the road herself."

"So you think it should be left to a woman to fight her rapist?"

David shakes his head. "What I think does not really matter."

"I thought that I could come here and maybe reason with you but now I see that there is no chance of that."

David raises a hand to stop him. He picks up the phone and dials a number. He waits a moment or two. "Good evening, could I speak to a Mr Ernest Robson? David Oswald!"

5.

Martin is standing over Maggie. "Why didn't you dance with me?"

"What?"

"You heard me. Why the fuck didn't you dance with me?"

Maggie looks confused.

"Fucking answer!"

Maggie kicks at him and gets him in the stomach. He lets out a gasp and stumbles back. Maggie lunges for the gun but he stamps at her. She rolls away and gets up. Martin gives a laugh and lunges at her. She gets behind the couch and he slashes at her. But she jumps back and makes a run for the door.

6.

Maggie is out in the hall and she sees the broken door, which has been closed over by Martin. She runs for it and he follows her out. She is close to making it.

7.

Maggie is standing in the large hall. The only other person in the room is Young Maggie, who is standing on the stage. "Maggie!"

8.

The vision is enough to slow Maggie down to realise that she cannot leave her daughter. Martin stabs at her and she veers to the side. He slams off of the door and Maggie starts running up the stairs, as there is nowhere else that she can go.

9.

Young Maggie has a gash on her head, but her eyes flutter open and she begins to laugh, lightly at first but it soon become quite creepy.

10.

Martin looks up the stairs and spits on Maggie's carpet. "I'm going to fuck you, then I'm going to kill you, then I'm going to fuck you again." He smiles. "And your daughter can watch."

He starts up the stairs.

11.

David is still on the phone. "I swear to you, Ernest, I am not lying. I am a friend of Maggie's and I think that even as we speak her life may be in danger." David listens for a moment. "You have to check it out. Could you take some officers there and go check it out?"

David nods as he listens. Andrew is watching.

"I'll meet you there if you like? I've helped the police before. You can check up on that if you want but you will be wasting valuable time. Thank you, Ernest, for listening to me. Goodbye."

David puts the phone down and stands up.

"So are we going to help Maggie?"

David shakes his head. "Not we! You're staying here."

Andrew shakes his head. "Like hell I am."

David takes out a gun from his pocket and points it at Andrew. "I hate these things, so don't make me nervous. I might kill you."

For someone who hates guns, David seems to hold this one quite well.

"I'm sorry, but if you come with me, then things might end up worse than they already are."

Andrew looks confused. "How could they be?"

"Maggie needs someone that she can love when all this is over. The last thing that I want to happen is Martin killing you. And if you go then that might just happen."

David ushers Andrew to a cupboard in the office. "Open it!"

Andrew opens it. It is empty, except for a few identical charcoal grey suits.

"Get inside."

Andrew gets in. David walks over and shuts it. He locks it and walks away. He puts the gun in his pocket.

12.

Maggie is against the door and Martin is throwing himself against it. She keeps being pushed away from it. She is terrified. He hits really hard and comes through and Maggie is sent flying onto the bed. Martin looks at her with angry eyes.

13.

Ernest comes out of his office. There are a couple of Policemen hanging about, not doing anything.

"You two come with me."

He looks at the duty officer.

"I want you to check up on a man called David Oswald. Find out what you can about him and get in contact with me."

"Yes sir."

Ernest and the two Policemen walk out.

14.

Martin is on top of Maggie and has ripped her blouse open, exposing her breasts. He roughly tweaks her nipples and she lets out loud gasps of pain.

"You fuck! You fuck! You fuck!" Martin screams.

His hands start wandering down to her crotch as he licks her face.

15.

Sheila is sitting reading a book. She looks at John. "Have you ever had that feeling that something horrible is happening?"

"I know what you mean." John replies.

Sheila drops her book.

16.

Martin cuts her underwear off of her, exposing her completely. He licks his lips. Maggie struggles but he puts the knife to her throat.

"You fuck! You fuck!"

17.

Keith lies on his bed, crying. He has a bottle of vodka lying on the bed beside him but it has not been opened. There is a smashed glass lying beside the bed. His feet are bleeding. He sniffs and wipes his nose as he cries.

"Maggie!"

18.

Martin is unzipping himself and fumbling. After a lot of trouble, he gets inside Maggie, who lets out a loud scream.

"You fuck!"

19.

Ernest is driving and the two Policemen are sitting in the back. He is going well over the speed limit.

"Are we in a hurry, sir?"

Ernest does not answer.

20.

Maggie is trying to struggle with Martin as he thrusts into her, but to no avail.

"Do you like to fuck? Is this the first fuck you've had in seven years? Got the seven years itch you little slut? You fuck!"

Maggie is crying and there are lines of blood at the sides of her mouth.

21.

Matthew and Lynn are kissing quite deeply when Lynn stops.

"What is it?"

He puts on a child like face.

"Don't you love me any more?" He asks.

Lynn gives a short laugh to signify that is not true then shakes her head. "I just have this weird feeling. I think that I should phone Maggie."

"Me sticking my tongue in your mouth made you think of Maggie?"

He stops and thinks about this for a second.

"Cool!"

22.

The phone beside the bed starts to ring and Martin grabs it with his knife hand. He just pulls it and the wire snaps out. He throws it against the wall. He does not even miss a thrust and Maggie seems to be drifting in and out of consciousness.

23.

Young Maggie is standing up. She walks over to the downstairs phone that is still ringing and picks it up. She does not speak to anyone but puts it back down again. She turns to the table.

24.

After smashing against the door a couple of times, Andrew spills out of the cupboard, falling to the floor. He is up in a few seconds and running for the door.

25.

Andrew gets outside and stands at an empty parking space.

"FUCKING BASTARD!" He screams.

26.

Sheila is in front of her husband. She is looking at him but once again there seems to be nothing. "Don't do this to me John. I can't be insane. I heard you talk."

27.

Maggie starts to regain consciousness again. Martin is thrusting into her quickly.

"Fuck me."

Maggie starts caressing him with her hands. He is obviously turned on by her saying this, maybe even more than the actual rape is exciting him.

"Fuck me."

She puts her hands on his trouser backside and seems to push him deeper inside her. She moves her hands slowly up his shirt back towards his head. He is groaning loudly as he continues to go deeper inside her. Maggie has started to moan too. She grabs a clump of his hair with both hands.

"Fuck me…"

She laughs.

"You fuck!"

She pulls his head back. He struggles. She head butts him, her forehead smashing off of his nose, making a horrible cracking noise. He gives a horrified scream as she pushes him off of her. She stands up beside him, suddenly feeling strong for the first time in as long as she can remember.

"Did that hurt?"

Martin has dropped his knife and is blindly searching for it. But the blood is everywhere and he is not succeeding. Maggie spits on him and kicks him in the ribs. He grabs her leg and she kicks him off of her. He gets up, regaining his composure.

"You'll fucking die for that."

Maggie backs away. But she has the fight in her now. She turns and sees Young Maggie standing at the door. She has the gun in her hand. Maggie snatches the gun from her and turns to Martin.

"Just who'll die, Martin?"

Martin laughs. "You don't have the guts."

Young Maggie is watching.

"She probably doesn't, which I think is quite commendable. But I do."

Young Maggie raises her empty hands as if she is clutching a gun. At the same time, Maggie raises her gun. Young Maggie swings round, so that she is facing a cupboard. But the swing causes Maggie to be aiming right at Martin. He starts to look worried. Maggie looks terrified.

"Bang! You're dead."

Young Maggie pretends to pull the trigger of her imaginary gun twice. Martin is shot in the throat and then in the head. Maggie screams. Young Maggie looks sad.

"I don't belong here. I should never have been born."

Maggie is shaking. "Who are you? What are you?"

"I am the part of you that Martin took away from you."

Young Maggie laughs.

"I am an abortion."

She swings her imaginary gun round. But this causes Maggie to be aiming right at her. Young Maggie pulls her imaginary trigger and Maggie hears gunshot. Her face contorts in terror as she realises what Young Maggie has made her do. She drops the gun and falls to the ground. She starts to cry. She looks down at the gun and picks it up. She puts it in her mouth. But when she pulls the trigger, all she gets are hollow clicks. She drops the gun again and starts to cry.

28.

David Oswald looks up at the bedroom window and his eyes drop down to his shoes. He looks sad as he turns and walks back to Andrew's car. He opens the car door as Police Sirens fill the air

THE END

www.ingramcontent.com/pod-product-compliance
Ingram Content Group UK Ltd.
Pitfield, Milton Keynes, MK11 3LW, UK
UKHW022116190726
13855UKWH00003B/881